STONY GLANCES

Other work by Peter Robins includes

Short Stories
  Undo Your Raincoats and Laugh
  Our Hero Has Bad Breath
  The Gay Touch (U.S.A.)
  Summer Shorts

Novels
  Easy Stages
  Survivors
  Touching Harry

Edited
  Doves For The Seventies
  Oranges and Lemons
  The Freezer Counter
  Fabulous Tricks (October 1991)

STONY GLANCES

Peter Robins

Third House (Publishers)

First published in February 1991 by Third House (Publishers)
69 Regent Street, Exeter EX2 9EG, England

World Copyright ©Peter Robins 1991

ISBN 1 870188 14 4

Photoset by Rapid Communications Ltd, Bristol BS3 1DX

Printed and bound by Billing & Sons Ltd, Worcester

Distributed in Europe by Turnaround, 27 Horsell Road, London N5 1XL

Cover design by Ruper Kirby

The cover painting by Alain Rosello, first exhibited at the St Jude's Gallery, Kensington, London, is entitled Dionysus Preparing To Fulfil His Promise. It is based on a myth better known in the Mediterranean than in England.

for Koos de Wilt and Ronald van Erkel

Above and well beyond Big Ben a plane threads among great banks of cumulus. Observing idly, waiting for its fuselage to re-emerge and glint in the hazy moonlight, Harry lets a cigarette stub drop into his plastic cup. A fizzle as it touches coffee dregs interests him no more than the occasional whirr from an automatic drinks dispenser whenever some other visitor treads quietly through the open door and, moments later, leaves without a word being exchanged.

Harry's energy is concentrated on his own irritation; on weeks of planning frustrated by one brief phone call. Not that he's worried about reclaiming part or even all of his air fare. That's for tomorrow's negotiations and/or row with the travel agent. It's the thwarting of his plans that irks him, a nagging persistent as toothache. Realising he'll need to make an intercontinental call to Harding, he checks the clock face on Big Ben. Only the earliest workers will be yawning into the streets of Sydney, he figures. Harding was never an early riser.

Sure that Paul Harding will offer commiseration about what's happened – and mean it – Harry does still wonder whether there'll be underlying doubts. For Harry, there's no question of the day's developments impeding his careful planning. At the least, what he's come to call his trial marriage with Australia would have to be delayed by a week or so. It's possible, he admits, that Harding might suggest unforeseen events were being used to conceal second thoughts.

Harry burps and wonders how long it will be before he can eat. His thoughts revert to Paul Harding. If the man doesn't understand that the callow and uncertain schoolboy, Harry Plimsoll, has disappeared with a final poem written twenty years back, then he's sunk into a blend of good Australian food and English sentimentality. More to the point, he's ignorant of a Harry Plimsoll determined to emigrate, leaving himself free of the whole damned chaos that life in London has become. What better than a trial marriage of a month down under? Harry congratulates himself on the way he's concealed his intentions in the editorial office. Who could question a free-lancer taking his well-earned vacation so far away, since there'd be the likelihood of the odd travel feature being mailed and no expenses charged? And, on return, questions about possible emigration would be no more than mechanical. Everything that had dove-tailed was now so neatly smashed. A few words on the telephone but effective as one blow with a sledge-hammer.

Without caring that he might not be the only occupant of the waiting room, Harry verbalises his anger.

–It's as if she guessed it. As though the old she-wolf blew my cover of a month-long assignment in Brussels.

Not yet ready to explore the long-term implications of the day's events, he runs over – for the umpteenth time – what he could have been doing in the next few days. It seems pointless already to remind himself that he should be relaxing in a plane while having such thoughts, rather than drumming fingertips on a window-sill and noting rain patter across the roofs of ambulances as they near the portico below him.

Harry has not allowed himself to romanticise Australia. There's been no dream of a waiting villa on the nicer side of Double Bay. Should such a dream have occurred, it would have been modified by an understanding that ideal houses have to be worked for. Even at forty-two, this doesn't daunt him.

Undisturbed by the occasional rumble of a hospital trolley along the stone floors of the corridor behind him, Harry runs over his unusual curriculum vitae: dishwasher, supply teacher, back-stage scene-shifter, bit-part actor in radio serials and always, as a last resort, humdrum clerical worker. It comforts him that a readiness to turn his hand to something new hasn't diminished.

Just for a moment, the chimes of Big Ben across the river distract him. He calculates he's been in the waiting room for more than an hour. Refusing to let this fuel his irritation, he compels himself to concentrate on something more appealing. Sydney after midnight – a whole new forest of quiet streets and waterside bars to be explored.

It might, he thinks, prove quite a challenge. Harding could be of little help. There'd be the pointing out of one beach as opposed to a dozen others, of course. A nicotined finger would be jabbed, as the car slowed at some intersection, towards one particular corner bar. All would be kindly meant: the least an old school-mate could do, etc, etc. Yet no help could rival Harry's own sixth sense cultivated through two decades, the trustworthy instinct that would guide him – as such an instinct had a thousand Harrys before him – towards a glade in a public park, a cove well distanced from the family beaches, or the least-lit of the bars by some deserted wharf.

At this point Harry's imagination falters. Doubts swirl through the bar he's visualising like a sea mist. Could Sydney – or San Francisco, or Cape Town come to that – offer more than an extension of the pattern he's constructed in London? Given the flattery of a perennial suntan; given, as well, some job that would tax his biceps more than a reporter's biro, he does have to accept that time is playing against him. King's Cross, Sydney, or King's Cross, London, it will be more difficult for him to pass for thirty-six much longer.

A search for his cigarette pack is at first unconscious. Finding his pockets empty, he searches round his feet. Impatience rises to near-hysteria until he recalls he's hidden the pack in a corner of the window-sill behind a Bible placed there, he assumes, by the hospital chaplain. Wondering why no one has thought to add a Torah or Koran, he flicks his lighter until there's a pimple of flame.

Sucking deeply at first on his cigarette, he re-examines the pattern of his private life in London. More of a roster is how he thinks of it. Three men in all: each equally satisfying and none too demanding. Curly-haired Mick tops the list with a game of darts first in a very ordinary bar and a very enjoyable hour in bed to follow. Harry keeps Mondays free for Mick, with the odd Thursday thrown in now and again.

And there's Bob.

Harry directs a smoke-ring towards the window-pane. Bob is enthusiastic but there have been little hints, building Wednesday by Wednesday, that this enthusiasm can't be limited to the double divan much longer. Small gifts are becoming a habit and there's been more than one reference to leaving the docks as containerisation takes over. Allusions to finding a room nearer Harry's place have not gone unnoticed. Musing on how satisfying nights with Bob have always been, Harry checks himself and sighs. There might have to be a new Wednesday man.

His thoughts turn to Gordon and he smiles. Gordon Laird is as winsome by sunlight as he is by the bedside reading lamp. Harry has always wondered if Gordon's caution in expressing physical delight adds to his charm. Though it's something they've never discussed, Harry suspects that Gordon might be seeking a deep and meaningful partnership. Were he to voice it, while looking at Harry with his grey-green eyes, it would be his last Friday.

Conscious of a sudden discomfort, Harry realises the cigarette is scorching his finger joints. He drops it, grinds it into the glossy parquet with his heel, and kicks it into a corner.

While continuing to lick his fingers, he notes the landing lights of what he knows can hardly be the same plane. This leads him to consider again how far Australia might offer solutions. Would it be anything more than a new roster? He calculates just how many years he might have left until the beach boys expected payment in cash or in entertainment. How long before he'd have to sit, waiting for slabs of beefcake to come looking for an approachable uncle? At least, by remaining in London, Mick, Bob and Gordon would continue to visualise him as they had at first glance. He doesn't doubt that. It does concern him more to speculate on how long he would find their first grey hairs and the deepening grooves around their mouths acceptable. Sexy as Mick, enthusiastic as Bob, tender as Gordon; how satisfying could any man be once his pubic hair began to grey and whiten?

The purposeful clip-clop of sensible shoes on polished stone intrudes until Harry can no longer ignore it. Some nurse, sister or matron is very surely heading for the waiting room. Muzzling his anger, he is forced to accept that Australia and almost everything else on his horizon seems to depend on solving the problem that's brought him, on a wet March evening, to a cheerless room garnished with hideous plastic daffodils.

There's no hesitation in the confident tread until whoever it is pauses, Harry presumes, in the doorway.

–Mr Plimsoll?

Thumbs up, or thumbs down, which will it be? For Harry, all else is secondary as he spins round, registers the professional smile of the young woman who faces him, and tries to interpret an answer from her eyes. Has the well-intentioned team working somewhere along the disinfected corridor been successful? A doctor with the build of a rugger full back had advised that they'd keep trying for a further thirty minutes before giving in gracefully. Harry recalls how curious the phrase had seemed. As though the gallant team would continue to attempt a joint seduction of the still figure on an operating table until conceding that they could not compete with the experience of that grey lover who cannot be rejected.

What, Harry wonders, would be the effect on the freckle-faced nurse were he to parry question with question? A start could be made by asking why they'd not done the sensible thing and let the old bitch go. With any luck that would shake all the values inculcated in her and shatter her confident smile.

He pulls his fists from his raincoat pocket.

–So, nurse, what's the news?

–I'm Sister Theatre, actually. Not that it's important. . .

Resisting a sweet-toned quip: something on the lines of Actually, my arse, you thin-lipped little careerist, Harry attempts a nervous pleasantry.

–Important for your pay packet, I should hope. Sorry. What are you here to tell me? Has she gone?

Sister Theatre's eyes soften. Harry has his answer. Efforts to control a groan tax him as, in a split second, a whole distasteful panorama opens for him.

–Your mother is a very tough old lady, Mr Plimsoll. . .

–I'm well aware of that, Sister. Fortunately – for me, I mean – it runs in the family.

Somewhat confused, Sister Theatre furrows her brow and notes Harry's phrase as one to be logged in Margaret Plimsoll's case history. She takes a couple of further steps into the room and fidgets needlessly with a miniature watch pinned to her starched apron.

–How interesting. Well, it's my job to tell you she's going to be all right. Intensive care for a couple of days, I expect. Then we'll give her a pacemaker. After that, we find, these old ladies can be as good as new. Some go on quite merrily to a hundred, Mr Plimsoll.

At best, the tone is firm; at worst, vicious. They both know that. Harry is already speculating. Could a pacemaker, like a dialysis machine, be turned off surreptitiously? Actions labelled humane or inhumane are irrelevant. To Harry, anything seems justified that might avert the sudden hell that gapes at his feet: Margaret, delighted at a resurrection and ready to torment all around her for another twenty years, gets religion. A not too fanciful script, Harry fears, since she will be recuperating among Irish Catholic nurses and Scottish Calvinist doctors. He has to restrain himself from shaking the dimpled chin of Sister Theatre while enquiring if she considers herself to be on the staff of a religious institution rather than a London hospital.

His own teeth almost rattle as he contemplates a very possible future. All his Sundays mapped out for him towards the horizon of his fiftieth birthday. He begins to predict the street-corner chatter of Margaret's neighbours: *Always a devoted son . . . comes to lunch each Sunday . . . hail or shine he passes my window on the stroke of one . . . Put the spuds on, I always say, there's Mr Plimsoll bringing the old duchess back from church. Isn't she a marvel for her age? . . .* His only refuge is corrosive irony.

–Well, isn't that splendid news? Another triumph for you all. . .

Sister Theatre works hard to conceal her dislike. She doesn't care for intellectuals who never seem to say what they mean. Moreover, she finds difficulty in connecting trendy sports wear, but a filthy buttonless raincoat, with someone on the editorial staff of one of England's nicer family magazines.

–Your mother's under sedation, as you'd expect, Mr Plimsoll. You could take a quick peek from the doorway . . . if you wish to.

–I think I'll leave all that until tomorrow, Sister. Tell me . . . did she know I was here?

–I'm sure she did.

A professional lie offered and accepted. Harry moves to a corner and picks up his umbrella.

–I wonder if you'd mind waiting a little longer, Mr Plimsoll?
–Something you need me to sign?
–Not at all. We can manage all that's necessary . . . Night Matron looked in a while back but she said you seemed to be

preoccupied. Very understandable, of course. Night Matron's read the hand-over notes about your mother. She mentioned to me that she'd like a word with you. I'm sure you'll be anxious to hear. Anyway, she shouldn't keep you too long. We usually suggest an early night for next-of-kin, too. The strain takes its toll, doesn't it?
–Seems I'll just have to starve for a bit longer. . .
–Goodnight, Mr Plimsoll. The news must be a great relief to you.
Without giving Harry the chance to reply, Sister Theatre nods in the direction of his chin and clip-clops away with her certainties intact.
Impotent fury sweeps across Harry like gusts of the March gales over Hungerford Bridge. As if surprised by them, his eyes water, but it is with anger. Again and again Sister Theatre's verdict buffets him: *a very tough old lady*.
Giving not one damn that the door's barely closed, he spits all the venom of his frustration at the vase of plastic daffodils.
–She's done it again. The old she-wolf has done it. Not even content with seeing most of us out. No. For Margaret Plimsoll, nee MacCawdie, husband, brothers, sisters, neighbours, two home helps and half a dozen lifelong friends are not enough. No. Now she lies, nourishing herself and gurgling like some infant on the breast of a respirator. And when they've weaned her from it, who's left for her to feast on? Winnie. Aunt Winnie, nutty as a fruit cake and stacking another sherry bottle behind the fridge . . . And me. Jesus H. Christ, the old predator could see me into retirement and my own first heart attack. She bloody could, and may well do . . . Margaret in her final role: muffled in black and stinking of mothballs, they trundle her out, noble and upright, to my own fucking cremation.
He blows his nose between pinched fingers. To a couple of passers-by, he hopes the sound he makes will seem one contemptuous and protracted fart. Wiping the snot on his fingers across a window-pane, he shouts a furious postscript.
–But not if I can help it, you won't. I'll see you out, you ravenous old bag of bones. If it's you or me against the wall, dear mother of mine, I'll bloody win, whatever the cost.
About to tear the daffodils from their vase and strangle each one

with his trembling hands, Harry hears another footstep, slower this time, but still hinting at a self-assurance that outstrips his own.

☆

Hands that stretch out quietly into the shadows do not distract the speaker for a moment. Once the table lamps have been switched on, Gordon Laird runs a professional eye along the bookshelves. He's less interested in the paperbacks than in the construction. Satisfied that it is a genuine Victorian piece, not a reproduction bought in the Tottenham Court Road, he shifts his focus to the student sitting two chairs to his right. To Gordon, both the speaker's face and body seem absurdly young when contrasted with the second-hand battle blouse.

Perhaps the fully-lit room, in which the student can see his temporary audience, accounts for a slight lowering of the voice. It does nothing to diminish his fervour and, Gordon notes, the arguments are reinforced with deliberate eye-to-eye contact around the circle. How far, Gordon wonders, are these restless glances based on thought-through convictions, and how much an uncertain statement of very recently acquired ideas? The tone is familiar enough to him, if not the concepts. There's an aggressive ring that evokes the gas-lit kirks of his childhood. In a fourth-floor London apartment he watches and hears the self-assured performance of someone convinced that he alone is custodian of the truth.

An uncontrollable smile erupts from Gordon's lips and he's forced to look down. Recollections of his own past glide into a teenage fantasy. He's sure that the downy-cheeked student, like many a young Scottish cleric with equally kissable lips, would be less rewarding than a plastic doll in bed.

Wondering what he himself will be able to say when it is his own turn to speak, he peeks furtively at his watch. Almost nine o'clock. The student has used two and a half minutes of his allotted five. His eyes on the speaker, Gordon makes a calculation. With luck, or even by inventing some bland excuse, he can be away within the hour and still meet Harry Plimsoll at the Hermes Tavern by ten forty-five. He folds his arms, assumes what he hopes will be taken for an encouraging smile not a sceptical twinkle, and listens.

–I just don't think we should take any of this shit. Right? . . . I mean, all this pair-bonding's fine. But we're talking about 1970. Yes? . . . Look around at any meeting like this one. Everyone's being so bloody genteel. Are you with me? What I've come here to say is, this pair-bonding is just subtle conditioning by the establishment. I mean, Freud was doing it back in history, wasn't he? . . . I see a brother over there waiting to intervene. I can guess what he's going to say. It's different for us . . . Am I right? Well, this is it. We must reject Freud. I mean, what else was he but a running dog for the bourgeoisie? All he ever wanted to do was to sit on his arse in Vienna and steer everyone back into controllable pairs eating cream cakes and conforming. You still with me? . . . Yes, brothers, we are different. So, if we're ever going to liberate ourselves – and I presume that's what it's all about – we've got to forget pairs and invent our own thing. Yes? What I'm really saying is, serial monogamy is out. Out. It's all nice and comfy playing substitute Mummies and Daddies but it's revisionism. And it's selfish. Our task is to go out from this hall tonight . . . this room . . . and start liberating others. Yes?

The student pauses for the first time as a batch of pamphlets slithers down his corduroys and across the fitted carpet. To cover his giggles, Gordon crouches to retrieve a few. All is as he suspected it might be. The Scottish chapel analogy holds. There will be pamphlets at the door and a challenge to spread the good news.

More flushed through his exertions than before, the student reseats himself and floods on.

–We must learn from the suffragettes. We must disrupt and demonstrate. Right? Don't we do it for Northern Ireland? And Vietnam? About time we did it for ourselves. Are you still with me? Let them arrest us. The media will just have to notice us in the end. Seeing us on the news, men like ourselves . . . men and women like ourselves, that is, will take heart. What I'm talking about are the hundreds of thousands of gays who live outside

London. They haven't even the shallow tolerance we enjoy. This is it. Somehow those lickspittles at Westminster have got to learn there's a whole sub-culture growing up. Forget them. They're dodos. It's a new decade. It's ours for the asking. Even here, in this room, I can sense things stirring. . .

Choking with laughter at the grossness of his own thought, Gordon feels tempted to murmur that nothing he's heard in the past few minutes has stirred his crotch. Yet he admits that here and there, like the odd nugget among a great deal of fools' gold, there's some sense in the young man's tirade.

–And we can learn from the Jewish people, too. Right? Support our own. Keep the cash flowing in the community. Use only gay electricians, gay travel agents, gay window cleaners. Right? And then it's on to the next step. Only elect onto our local councils men – and women, of course – who are willing to come out. After that, it's on to Westminster. Can we make a start tonight? Shall we say no more timid pairs hiding in the corners like mice? This is what it's about . . . Yes, Mr Convenor, I'm finishing . . . And my message is: Come Out. Whoever you are, wherever you are: Come Out.

Gordon stares down at the holes punched in his suede shoes. A weakness for satire which Blair had always sworn would be his downfall bubbles like champagne. He's tempted to ask the student whether the verbal cascade to which they've all been subjected is the best he can manage nowadays in the way of an orgasm. Only a deeper vein of kindness to a young man as idealistic as Blair had been when they'd first met tempers his scepticism.

Once he has made this comparison, Gordon finds it impossible not to contemplate how age and experience set him apart from the student. What point would there be in telling the young man of the harrassment and filth Blair and he had endured for ten years in Glasgow before making south? To itemise envelopes of shit on the doormat, graffiti sprayed on the door itself, and Saturday nights when the choice had become a few beers in front of the television or a beating-up on the way home from the pub, would be to invite a sharp reminder that this was a new decade and one in which new ideas stirred.

Nor does Gordon need anyone to challenge his reason for

attending the meeting. He is looking for someone who'll respond to his own willingness to share the coming years in an ongoing way: something he would like to think Harry Plimsoll might offer. It is an awareness that he's already investing too much and too quickly in his friendship with Harry that's prompted him to glance, at least, elsewhere. Not that he's impressed with those who surround him at the meeting. Indeed, he considers pleading an urgent need to leave. Having scanned the dozen faces in the room he's compelled to side with the student in one respect. They are complacent. And about as challenging as slices of Edam cheese.

Too late for a discreet exit. Gordon's immediate neighbour, a man in his late twenties whose grey flannels tremble so much that they ruffle Gordon's jeans like a breeze, is already speaking.

–Name's Dave. Not sure I should be here, really. What I mean to say is, I wouldn't bet on being welcome next time. . .

This elicits sympathetic gestures and murmurs of encouragement.

–No. Hang on a bit. I mean that . . . It's like this, see? . . . I'm adopted. Leastways, I was. Me step-mum couldn't have no more of her own. She'd had two already . . . older than me, naturally. Don't get me wrong. I was accepted. One of the family, like, from the word go.

Anyrate, Syd . . . he was me eldest step-brother. He was always, well, like a hero to me, see? . . . Anyrate, we started messing about together when Syd was twenty and I'd have been close on thirteen. Seemed natural enough, him being in the next bed and me starting to have wet dreams. First off, it was just larking about. Playing with one another's cocks . . . Having competitions to see who could shoot first or highest up the vinyl wallpaper. We'd do it most nights . . . unless he was too shagged out from the building sites.

He was warm, was Syd. Good body, too. We used to do the weights together. Syd taught me a lot. After that, it got to cycling trips up the river. Just days out, first off, then weekends . . . One night we was in our tent. August it was, so we had the flap up for a breath of air. That night was special, see? . . . We didn't have a stitch on, neither of us. Didn't matter. We was by

ourselves in a hayfield, and there was nothing over the hedge but the river, so who cared?
Anyrate, I expected the usual pattern . . . bit of wrestling first . . . me giving in, and the rest following, like. It was different that night, though. Not saying I didn't enjoy it. Far from it. . .
Syd leaned right down on me when he'd got me pinned to the sleeping bag. Nothing was said. Not a dickie bird. Just kissed me on the mouth, did Syd, gentle as a dove. I won't never forget that. . .
Point is, all that was more than going through a phase for me. Me step-mother called things that: a phase. I heard her say it after Dad sent Syd away. Heard her through the door. They'd found out, see? . . . And I knew when. Bound to come out, wasn't it, us all being in a council block with walls like cardboard. .?
It was like this. I'd had to put a hand over Syd's mouth one night. I knew bloody fine Dad was listening on the landing after he'd used the toilet. Thing is, Syd was just about coming and he didn't care. The old bed was creaking away and I couldn't stop Syd shoving quicker. We'd always use a bit of hand cream so I'm not saying he was hurting. He never would have, with me . . . Only the first time it hurt. Just a bit . . . Cared about me, did Syd. Not that I saw him again after Dad sent him packing. Never believed their yarn about Australia, mind. He was here in London. I knew that. You could say I'm still looking for him, even today. Made a start by getting a place of me own, see? I was twenty myself, then.
I know that's all history, if that's what you're thinking. Course it is . . . Right now, I'm working on the buses. Got a room down Tooting way . . . And there's the problem. The landlady's a widow. She lets, and does a bit of part time at the new launderette on the corner. Point is, she's got a lad of her own. Fair dotes on me, does Sean . . . I know we've got some clever blokes here tonight so I bet you've worked it out for yourselves. If you need telling, Sean's fourteen. . .
Gordon is among those who do guess what's likely to come next, and he's able to concentrate on reactions to Dave's story. The student is plainly startled as though confronted with evidence he's never expected to have to examine. There's a sympathy

in the eyes of a man of more than sixty but – here and there – Gordon catches symptoms of agitation. Worried glances sweep the room seeking confirmation in others of their own unease.

There'll be an outburst. Gordon's sure of that. He senses a heightening tension that must be dispersed in speech or action. There's the whiff of aggression that Blair once taught him to detect on the terraces at Ibrox and Murrayfield. He rather expects it will be the student who will explode first.

Gordon is wrong. The intrusion comes from a man much Gordon's own age. As Dave risks a shy look round the circle, Gordon notices a pair of knuckles opposite growing white and bloodless as they grip an expensive raincoat.

–Mr Chairman . . . well, Convenor then, or whatever. It so happens I've risked perhaps rather more than most by coming here tonight. As I mentioned, I did not – for reasons that were understood – reveal my own name. One breath of scandal and my career . . . snigger if you wish, not all of us are student revolutionaries today and conforming diplomats tomorrow . . . One breath of scandal and my chances in the media would be in ruins. I say chances advisedly, Mr Convenor. In a quiet way, and that is the way England works, I had hopes I might influence opinion about people like us. Most of us, that is. There is little I can do for a child molester other than point him in the direction of a clinic. Whatever my sympathies for Dave personally, there is, in my view, no way that we can carry him . . . or anyone like him. . .

The convenor, a mild man with horn-rimmed glasses and a pleasant North Midlands accent is not in any way thrown by this forceful outburst. Once the protester has paused, eager to gauge the impact of his intrusion, the convenor reminds him that everyone has to be given the courtesy of a hearing. The media man has had his and Dave must be allowed the same.

–I'm sorry, Mr Convenor. That is not good enough. Either Dave leaves this room or I do.

To Gordon, if not to anyone else, it is obvious that Dave is beyond tears. He is withdrawing further into himself with every critical phrase. Were he able to curl into a ball, Gordon imagines he would do just that: a tiny globe of misery that cannot be comforted.

Noting embarrassment everywhere, Gordon judges it to be the moment to speak.

–If Dave leaves, he'll not go alone. My name is Gordon Laird and I wish to hear the rest of what he has to say.

As Gordon intends, the media man accepts this as a challenge to the authority with which he feels his trade invests him.

–Then, do we take it, Mr Laird, that you are of a like persuasion?

–You can take what you bloody well like. I'll hear Dave's story here, or I'll hear it at the nearest bar . . . May Dave continue, Convenor?

The answer's no more than a brief nod, for the convenor is urging the media man to remain. It's a lost cause. Raincoat over his arm, briefcase gripped by white knuckles, the director, or editor, or whoever he is, walks with over-emphasised dignity to the door and does not bother with the niceties of goodbyes.

–Well, I expected that, even if none of you did. Not much more to say anyway. I can see how that gentleman with the briefcase felt. . .

Dave falters into silence until Gordon, with a nudge, encourages him to finish his tale.

–All right then. Young Sean's fourteen, like I said. Nothing's happened yet, I swear it. He gets this dreamy look in the eyes at bedtime now. Bought himself a body building mag a few weeks back. Left it on my divan. And he keeps hinting, too, about a trip to the Lake District. Bought some maps, he has. His mum's just got him a new racer, see? . . . It'd have to be in August . . . August again, eh? It's me'd be playing Syd this time, though, wouldn't it? . . . That's it then. But there's one question I'd like to ask. . .

–Questions after coffee, please.

Dave gets up.

–Yeah, well, I won't be staying, thanks all the same. Just wanted to ask this student here if he'd have me marching by him round Trafalgar Square. I'm not asking for an answer, see? Anyway, thanks, all of you, for listening. See you on the number eighty-eight.

Once more the convenor tries to protest but there's little support. People are suddenly interested in the bookshelves, or in a David Hockney line drawing above the radiator.

Gordon also gets up.

–I'll need to be going, too. Not that I'm too shy to talk. Maybe another time. It so happens I've a date. Close to Trafalgar Square, would you believe? . . . Anyway, I'll walk you to the bus, Dave.

They clatter down the uncarpeted stairs without a word said. In the porch they stand buttoning raincoats for the drizzle has started again.

–Was that you having them on, Gordon, about meeting someone? Bit of a bolshie Scotsman are you?

–I do have a date. His name's Harry. Folk like that do make me bolshie. Come on, I'm not pressed for twenty minutes. I could do with a drink and so could you.

The bar is half deserted. Either the landlord or the brewery seems to be unaware of the need to meet changing demands. There's no television suspended in a corner. No one has installed a pool table, and there's no sign of a local pop group or an amateur drag act.

Glasses are touched but nothing's said for more than a minute. Gordon stares at Dave's head bent over the table. The fair hair is thinning early as Blair's had done. Dave's stubby fingers hold the beer tankard gently. Gordon sums Dave up as a man without violence; one who's honest, bewildered, and very much alone.

–It's like this, Gordon. I'm not so good with words as most of them there tonight. Leastways, not about personal things. . .

–I'll second that. I'm not so keen myself on dancing naked over the coffee table in strange company. No, it's not my scene at all.

Dave looks puzzled.

–Not trying to say you're like me, are you? Is it boys with you as well? Not in general, I mean. See how I trip myself up? I meant, do you have a boy who's special?

Gordon's laugh is gentle and uncomplicated.

–No. Not at all. I'm not saying I'm with you, but I wasn't against you back there. You surely guessed you'd be an embarrassment to most of them?

–Shouldn't ever have gone in the first place. Seemed a chance just to natter for once. Doesn't happen often for a bloke like me. I shouldn't have bothered. . .

–Not at all. They needed their eyes opened. Not the convenor. You might go back sometime and see him. A good man. For the rest of them, don't bother. I'll not. . .
–Gordon, you sure you're not trying to tell me something? . . . Here, let me get us another pint . . . You kinky or something?
Gordon laughs again, this time in an uninhibited way. The barman, glancing from his evening paper, smiles as if regretting he's not in on the joke.
–Me? Kinky? . . . Now you mention it, Dave, I guess some of that gang might have thought so. I would have said, if I'd stayed, that I lived with another man, first in Glasgow, then here in London for eighteen years in all. I loved him. I still do . . . We gave little thought to growing older. None at all to accidents. We'd a small boat, you see, and we sailed most weekends at the mouth of the Thames. One Sunday, a squall . . . we capsized . . . Blair was drowned. Sometimes I think it might have solved a lot if I had been, too.
–Christ, that's awful, Gordon. . .
–Blair's death or my own dark wish? Maybe you're wondering why I was there tonight. It seemed a chance. Maybe I'd meet someone I could take to and who'd fancy me. Someone with a bit of basic warmth, you understand? I'm not saying I could hope to replace Blair . . . That'd ask too much of anyone . . . But the warmth, Dave. That's basic. If that's lacking, I'd as soon have a slab of cold beef on the next pillow. And if that makes me an outsider like you, so be it. We'll drink to outsiders with that pint you've been threatening.
When Dave returns from the bar, they toast each other with easy grins and little is said until Gordon, noticing the wall clock, calculates he'll need to leave within minutes if he's to make the Hermes as promised. Although he anticipates another enjoyable night with Harry Plimsoll, Gordon does wish he could pop a little of Dave's uncomplicated honestly into his pocket and implant it in Harry, who so often appears remote, and occasionally to be playing a part in some drama for which only he has the script.
–I'd a thought while you were at the bar, Dave. We might meet again . . . say next week. . .
There's the hint of a shadow across Dave's light blue eyes as he

seeks the motive for this simple invitation. Expecting to reassure him, Gordon leans to touch the lightly-downed wrist with an index finger. Dave's hand is withdrawn as though molten steel had seared his flesh. The fear in his eyes is unmistakable.
–What for?
–For a drink, man. I'm not a copper out to trap you for names and addresses. . .
–Didn't say that, did I?
–What then?
For a second time, Dave is contracting into a tight, small sphere of misery.
–What you want with me, Gordon? What you after?
–For the third time: a drink. No more. I've no designs on you. It'd take me a long time to look fourteen again, wouldn't it? And I'll never be a hero like your step-brother, Syd . . . So, now, what d'you say to next Wednesday?
–I'll have to think about that.
–Do. Wednesday, I'll be here. A meeting of the Outsiders Club, eh? No. Let's make that the Outside The Outsiders Club. That's what we are, Dave. Neither of us so good at giving the concrete glances these Londoners seem to specialise in. Now I must go. . .

☆

Knowing he'll never make the Hermes Tavern, and shrugging aside the fact that he'll be standing Gordon up, Harry concentrates on essential needs: food, and a little solitude to mull over his predicament. The visitors' canteen – wherever it might be – will long since have shut. The most that can be expected from machines in the Casualty Reception area, he guesses, will be crisps or chocolate bars and an endless supply of plastic cups overflowing with a cross between powdered coffee and brown soup.
He's compelled to accept that a bag of fish and chips is about all that South London is likely to offer.
And then?

Harry's glance along the riverside that spreads from east to west beyond the rain-spattered window is perfunctory. He assesses the terrain with an experienced eye, having had years to refine his strategy. He can read the behavioural codes of those who linger by the all-night coffee stalls with a skill that would be envied by any spy-catcher. As he weighs the choice between setting out on his hunt at Westminster, or making a quick call at the Greasy Spoon café by the corner of Fleet Street, a mellow voice tinged with amusement interrupts him.

–Mr Plimsoll . . . Harry?

The use of his first name prompts him to wheel sharply and face the door. Hopes soar as he perceives a woman obviously more senior than a nurse. The short blue shoulder-cape and matching frock imply status. Can it be a member of staff noted for her tact in coping with the bereaved? He rather hopes so. In fact, he begins to construct a suitable speech for her . . . *A sudden relapse, I'm afraid . . . She battled valiantly but then slipped easily away . . . A peaceful end, Mr Plimsoll. Such things can happen . . . We'd have no objection to a quick funeral. Day after tomorrow suit you? . . . The Almoners' office will give you a cover note for your travel agent . . . No reason why you shouldn't be in the arms of a tangy surfer within a week . . . Now, Harry, a cup of tea, just the two of us?*

His second glance at the well-rounded but not stout woman much his own age causes Harry a moment's disturbance which he cannot place. She is, after all, considering him with something more than a professional look.

–Forgive me, Sister. I was miles away. . .

–Australia perhaps? I'm going on the notes they sent up from Casualty. Well, that's as may be. You clearly don't recognise me. . .

–Should I? Medical journalism's not my field . . . My own health is disgustingly good. So . . . ?

The woman moves further into the room so that light from the yellowed plastic strip in the ceiling defines her more sharply.

–If your thoughts weren't on Australia, shouldn't think they were on your own past. Try pushing the years back a bit. Harry Plimsoll at seventeen. Remember a party before you went to college? . . . Of course, if you'd bothered to keep Noreen Humby's photograph, it might. . .

–Never! Jesus, I just don't believe this! Noreen from the Convent Girls' High working here . . . Listen, you're not dressed like the others. Are you on the Welfare side by any chance?
–No, Harry. I'm an Assistant Matron.
Pulling out his cigarette pack, Harry offers one. Noreen declines with a wave of her fingers that's permissive rather than admonitory.
–Noreen Humby! Who'd have thought you'd have battled out of the suburban mists? I'm not being patronising. What I mean is, Noreen, you always seemed to be so ready for early nesting. What about the Canadian mountie? Did you marry him?
–The mountie with the bounty? . . . Yes, we had the full bit, white wedding despite clothing coupons. . .
–I wondered about it, once or twice. Never went back to the Thames Valley myself, as you'll know. The odd bits of gossip came from Paul Harding and Sue. All that stopped when they split up. Paul said you just disappeared. Did you elope with the mountie . . . the moonlight flit?
–Not exactly. Everyone was against him: Mum, Dad . . . even Paul and Sue. I sometimes think that's half the reason I did it. The break for independence . . . bit later than yours.
–Good for you. Did they send search parties in pursuit? Huskies?
–He and I were ready for all that. Not for the same reasons, as it turned out. Guess what I did? I got other nurses at the West Middlesex to send cards for me whenever they went on leave. That threw everyone off the scent. Posted my own, of course, once we were in America. No address though. . .
With a sigh, Noreen sits and indicates that Harry should do so but he prefers to remain standing with his back to the window.
–What's the sigh for? You regret what you did?
–Wouldn't say that . . . Maybe just sending cards out of the blue. Maybe that . . . Now it's my turn to receive them. . .
–Explain. . .
–Another time, perhaps. You could drop in for a sherry when I'm next on duty, if you like. So, what about you, Harry?
–So, what about me?
The twinkle of amusement at the corners of Noreen's eyes resurfaces. She tries to conceal this recognition of Harry's instant

defensiveness. That has not changed in a quarter of a century. Looking at him, it is Harry's father that Noreen thinks of, not his old empire-builder of a mother, Margaret, snoring just this side of death's doorstep no more than three minutes' walk from where they are talking. Noreen can still visualise John Plimsoll's closed features, parrying enquiries with only a fiddling of the thumbs to betray unease. Like father; like son, she thinks.
–Harry, what's all the defensive bit? . . . What we all wanted to know was whether you found someone at college. In Wales, wasn't it?
–Yes. As a matter of fact, I did.
–Didn't last?
–Lasted long enough for me to discover the kind of relationship that suits me. . .
–Dear God! You sound like one of the day courses we have to attend. In plain English, did you get married?
Tapping his cigarette on the rim of a plastic cup, Harry considers his reply. For one long and appalling instant, he wonders if Noreen might have hopes of a middle-aged romance. The teenage sweethearts reunited at last. Although it's not been specified, he's sure she's divorced, not merely separated from the Canadian. What more alluring, before the menopause and a gentle autumn, than a discreet affair to break the tedium of a work roster?
Noreen anticipates some ambiguity in Harry's answer. For her, there'll still be doubt as to whether this will be merely characteristic of the man, or a concealment of something she has always suspected.
–Marriage didn't come into it, Noreen. Never has . . . for me. . .
–Scared of the risks, eh? So, what's it been, the Don Juan routine? Love 'em and leave 'em?
–Wrong. If you want a reference point, Tennyson would be better. Better to have loved and lost than never to have loved at all . . . Anyway, there's no one particular at present. What's more, I'm not on the lookout, either.
He regrets his emphasis on the last few words. Noreen, noting it, laughs.
–I was offering a glass of sherry, Harry. No need to bring a

bodyguard . . . You know, I can't recall if it was Sue or Paul said it, after you'd gone to Wales, I mean. Sue, I expect. Paul would have played the male solidarity bit. Sue said you'd never marry. I think she was right.
She wonders how he might react. Whatever else, Noreen knows she can dismiss the mother and neutered son syndrome. Instead, she surveys buttons missing on his raincoat and unironed creases in Harry's shirt. She deduces that he lives alone. Yet who, she speculates, stays overnight from time to time?
—You can think what you like about that. Maybe I'll tell you some day. Right now, I'd say we ought to be having a word about the prognosis for my mother.
Content to let him win the point, Noreen stands up and smooths her frock down over her hips.
—Very well, Harry. Let's not bother with the sales talk. Basically, the will to survive is there. Very strong it is, too. They told you we've been coping with the second heart attack? That's the biggie always. Good thing she had it here after admittance. . .
—Fortunate for her. . .
Noreen raises her eyebrows and flicks a spot of cigarette ash from her cape.
—That's the way the wind blows, is it? Can't say I'm amazed. You and your mother always seemed to be heavily into your own private war . . . Anyway, your domestic arrangements in the future aren't my concern. You should reckon on her being here another three weeks. And then, Harry, you'd better be prepared for her to toddle on for anything up to another decade. . .
—So it's true? . . . What your Sister Theatre said?
—Quite true. Margaret'll get a pacemaker in a matter of days. Old Sybil Thorndike has one, you know. Look at her, bouncing around the West End like a twenty-year-old.
Less concerned with the good health of an octogenarian actress than with Margaret's likely interference in his own future, Harry's frustration surfaces. His eyes harden and he pounds the fist of one hand into the palm of the other.
—Right. You've been plain with me. My turn now, Noreen. I will not be recruited as an unpaid member of the bloody National Health Service. That's flat and you can tell your colleagues. And,

another thing, they'll get less than nowhere by playing the moral blackmail card against me. Don't bother with all that shit about rejecting my own mother. I've paid my health stamp like the rest and I expect to hear she's being coped with in return. . .
–Do calm down, Harry. You were always more of a socialist than the rest of us. So happens my own mother's still alive. I know a bit how you feel. We've got plenty of care services that'll cope with Margaret . . . at the moment. . .
–What's that supposed to mean?
–Well, just thank your stars this is happening now. I'll give you a tip as a journalist. The money's starting to dry up. We can see it on the wards, you know. Things'll be different in twenty years when we're facing a pension, I can tell you. Shouldn't think it'll make an ounce of difference if it's Sailor Ted or that crafty old tap-dancer Wilson running things over the bridge.
–That's all very interesting, I'm sure. You're not here to give me the soft soap? Sweetening me up before unloading her on me?
–Would a nervous hysteric be good for our patient? Think not. Calm down, Harry. Get a decent night's sleep and, as I said, drop by the office when I'm next on duty. Why not next Tuesday, after you've done your dutiful son visit?
–Thank you, Matron, and goodnight.
–Now just shut up. Whoever's Duty Sister on Balaclava will show you where I am. We'll have a laugh. It'll cheer up my last shift before my spring leave. . .
–Off to pick Cornish daffodils? A healthy ramble in the Welsh hills?
–Don't be so bloody patronising. I take my breaks on a Greek island. Might just tell you more about all that – and him – when I see you. Come on. I'll walk you to the stairs.
There is a calmness at the core of his one-and-only girlfriend that soothes Harry, despite his resistance and his determination not to be comforted. Her blend of common-sense and steadiness, topped up with humour, is something he's not found in any of the men with whom he has – from time to time – attempted to build more than a pleasant weekend.
–How do you stand it all, Noreen? The tedium, I mean, rosters . . . and bedpans. . .
Noreen laughs.

–Simple. Set my sights on what's achievable. No mystery in that. If you mean, how's my love-life, that's not difficult, either. Romance went with the mountie. Dimitri is enough. No Adonis, but he suits me . . . Hold on, we'll glance in on Margaret. By the way, who's your cousin, or her cousin, Alastair?
–There isn't one. Not that I know of.
–Odd. Your mother mumbled something about Alastair from Scotland being her next-of-kin if you couldn't be found. Might be a childhood memory. Violent upsets of the system often throw up forgotten memories . . . Now, no talking. I'll slide the door open. She'll look pretty pathetic.
Harry's fingers stray to the pockets of his raincoat. His hands plunged in, he closes his fists in strangleholds on his cigarette pack and his monthly travel pass.

☆

–*Another* drunken Scotsman!
–Fuck off, y'screaming painted queen.
This cool exchange of pleasantries occurs at the intersection of the Strand and Waterloo Bridge just as the clock on the spire of St Clement Danes has struck midnight. Gordon Laird, impervious to heavy rain coursing through his hair and onto the back of his neck, has not bothered to button up the collar of his raincoat. He wastes no energy on turning to confront the figure that has just flitted against him. If it reminds him of anything, it is of an outsize grey bat sweeping towards Trafalgar Square in a voluminous plastic mac, topped by a particularly spiky umbrella. The incident does check his flow of thought, however, and he takes shelter in the doorway of a clothing shop.
For much of the past hour he's been prey to a mixture of anger and self-pity and his mood doesn't alter as he stands watching the rain perform small arabesques in over-full gutters. His anger is directed equally at Harry Plimsoll and himself. He considers he's been taken in by yet another glib Londoner. It's obvious to Gordon that he's deluded himself by reading more into their couple of meetings than a weekend fling. He feels, yet again,

he's back to square one. And then common sense reminds him of what he'd come to accept in the months following Blair's death: starting out afresh at thirty-nine would not be easy. Once he's reached this point, a touch of wry humour intrudes on his self-pity. Not for the first time he asks himself just how many frogs he'll need to kiss before he finds a prince – at least in embryo – on the adjacent pillow.

As he contemplates the rain that spurts from trucks making north from the bridge towards Covent Garden, his anger surges once more and he grinds his teeth. To have been given a false phone number had been no big deal. Little more than one of the risks of the game. But to have been given a disused line by Harry, who'd seemed so honest, even taken him to lunch with his old mother; that hurt.

Rain on his fingers dampens the cigarette he's lit, making it almost impossible to smoke. Between sucking on it angrily, he addresses it as though the object were Harry Plimsoll himself in miniature.

–A sexual highwayman, that's what y'are. No doubt laughing y'r head off this minute at a simple Scot . . . Bloody con-man. Well, what else are y'? All that glib chat about any worthwhile relationship needing to go slowly? I've been fobbed off with a load of bollocks, and we both know it. Y'r good on the words. I'll admit that . . . Not wanting to meet too often at the start to make sure each hug is as tender and thoughtful as the first. What was all that but crafty sales chat, eh? . . .

I see it all clear enough now. There was one thought in y'r scheming head. One . . . Off with my jeans and Gordon Laird'd serve as well as a hot water bottle to fend off the winter cold. I've been used . . . and I feel soiled. . .

Christ, do I miss you, Blair Brodie! We were right about these Londoners today. They skid from bed to bed, feeling less and less. Like a cook's fingers, they are, feeling no burns after a couple of months. And that goes for Harry the highwayman . . . He'd best not come round here tonight, or I'll do a little desensitising. . .

Always said I was naif in some matters, didn't y', Blair? . . . But not dumb. Oh, no, Harry Plimsoll. Not dumb. Cunning bastard, taking me to meet the old lady. What was that about? She with

her heather-in-the-gloaming picture of Scotland . . . No doubt she'd think the Gorbals was another Highland dance. All her blether about me reminding her of a dead relative. . .
Y'd a good teacher in her, Harry. Words flowing from the two of y's thick as this bloody rain . . . Drown y'rself in them, Harry . . . There's more fish in this mucky river than you. And maybe they don't all stink. . .
–Not talking about my feet, I should hope.
Panicked by the notion that his soliloquy, having been overheard by a stranger, might be interpreted as evidence of loneliness touching on eccentricity, Gordon becomes taciturn in an instant.
–What the hell d'you want?
–This a public doorway or a confession box? I want out of this pissing rain for a minute or two. Any objections?
To Gordon, the newcomer appears more dishevelled than himself. The young man, wearing only a thin denim jacket, is well soaked. His suede boots, whatever their original shade, are blackened through tramping the streets for some hours. In the shadows of the doorway, his hair seems thick veins of black against a marble forehead.
–Stay or go. It's of no importance to me. Get one thing straight. Y'can hear I'm a Scot. I'm not up for the big match. I live in this concrete jungle so I know all the sales chat, laddie. Don't come the few-pence-for-a-cup-of-tea nonsense with me. . .
–Don't need to. And I'm not laddie, I'm Fred.
Gordon looks at the newcomer with some curiosity and his stare is returned. Fred's chin has not been shaved for a couple of days and the stubble, unlike his hair, is nut-brown. Gordon picks on this detail and magnifies it to a symbol of down-and-outness, even though the eyes are at odds with Fred's general appearance. The glance is firm, not broken and reduced to pleading by a cycle of bad luck.
Fred, of course, is in no position to remind Gordon of those days, sometimes weeks, when the depression following Blair's death had so maimed him that he had sprawled, drunk and unwashed, on a wreath of bedding that flowered with shit and sperm.
–I've no interest in who y'are or why y'r here.

–Quite the hard bastard, eh? Someone been giving you a bad time?

Gordon lights another cigarette but does not offer one to Fred.

–My business is my business. What are y' after?

–Me? Nothing. Just thought you might fancy a change from arguing with yourself. . .

In the momentary flash of a truck's headlights, as it eases forward from the traffic lights, Gordon notes the upturn of Fred's lips into a puckish smile as he scores this hit. A direct reply is difficult.

–Not that it's of concern to anyone other than me, but I've not met a soul worth opening my lips to these past two hours. . .

–Cheer up, Jock. Your luck's changed. . .

It's an overture. Gordon is sure of that. As to whether it is no more than the easy-going cameraderie of those who find themselves alone on the streets after midnight or the more specific approach of someone intent on sharing a bed, he can't decide. His own response disturbs him. He's torn between two impulses: both extreme. He could, without moving three paces, hug Fred and even dare a kiss on the lips that are more generous than weak. On the other hand – and this really worries him – he's just as inclined to lash out, with fists that have already begun to harden, at that same mouth for having so boldly started to chat him up.

The first is more than Gordon dares. The alternative? He's still sober enough to realise it would be no more than a chance to level the score with Harry Plimsoll. So he contents himself with a glare.

–And you're my lucky penny? Give it a rest. We've nothing in common. I'm close on forty and you're still milky behind the ears. Your world's all pot and pop and revolution. Me, I can't tell the difference between this week's hit tune and *The Bluebells of Scotland* . . . And I don't care for either.

–You must care for something. We could talk about that. Anyway, I'm twenty-four . . . nearly. What's your real name, Jock?

–Does it matter? . . . Oh, I get the picture. The two of us sit here on the kerb like two lost babes in the wood, eh? We spend the night swopping tales of this city and its stony-eyed folk. That it?

–Doesn't have to be that way. . .
–Does it not? Well, you find someone else to chat with. My night bus'll be along in five minutes. I've a job to go to in the morning, even if you haven't. . .
As Gordon speaks, Fred watches him from under wet eyelashes. He wonders if the Scotsman, who's plainly more lonely than himself and seems to have taken a hard knock recently, is trying in a roundabout way to invite him back. Having lived on his wits in a dozen cities during the past three years, Fred has learned to spot what he calls England's emotional paralytics. He's rather proud of this phrase and intends to amuse his mother with it one day.
–So happens I'm going to fix a job tomorrow, Jock.
–Good luck with it. You'd best get some sleep first, I'd say. That's my intention. . .
Fred tries as gentle a prompting as he can.
–And . . . ?
–I'll be catching the bus by myself. That clear?
On balance, Fred decides it's better to let Gordon howl for company alone. There's violence near the surface in the Scotsman, though Fred gauges it would be verbal. He's a little disappointed for he finds the man attractive because he taps a spring of caring that Fred has recently discovered in himself. A pity, but Fred consoles himself with a reminder that it's still early enough to make for the riverside coffee stall where he's no doubt there'll be less unpredictable company.
–It's clear enough, Jock . . . What if I'm taking the same bus?
This last, half-hearted move is accompanied by Fred's impish smile. It's not lost on Gordon. His tongue dries with apprehension on the roof of his mouth. He swallows nervously, steeling himself to offer an invitation. And then he falters. The outcome at best could be no more than another meaningless one-night stand. At worst he'd be tempted to play Harry Plimsoll, leading Fred on and then teaching him – the bitter way – not to be so trusting.
–The odds are against it, Fred. If that's y'r name. . .
–Why the hell should I lie to you?
–Got a birth certificate to prove it? This place is full of conmen. . .

–You're different, of course?
–Watch it, laddie. Yes, I am different. . .
–I'd say you're a bit of a casualty, Jock. Someone's really pissed you off. You reckon I'm trying to pick you up, or something?
–I'd not find it astounding. . .

Despite the realisation that his shoes are letting water in and that he's cold from head to toe, Gordon feels a rush of warmth through his body. He knows he wants Fred but cannot bring himself to ask.

–Wouldn't you, Jock? You're wrong, mate. I'm not on the game. Look, there's your bus. Have a good night with your monsters. . .
–What are you cracking on about now?
–You should know. Having a duel to the death with one of them when I turned in here.
–I don't need your help in coping with them. Or anyone's.
–Suit yourself. I could stand you a hot drink. . .
–There's hot drinks at home.
–As I said, suit yourself. Pity. . .
–What's a pity?
–I'll tell you, Jock. Pity all that warmth deep down in you only comes out all poisoned. Like stinking pus.
–Listen. D'you fancy me? I'm not used to being chatted up by rent boys. . .
–And I'm not used to being insulted by fucking neurotics . . . Just piss of, will you? I've got your number, mate . . . Fancy me like a Christmas dinner, you do. Don't kid yourself . . . Go on, piss off home and have a slow, safe wank. . .

The aim of Gordon's fist is less sure than it would have been, had he not been drinking for two hours. Fred dodges, throws back his head with a chuckle, and scampers off into the night singing *We'd lead the life we choose, We'd fight and never lose* until he's no more than a fuzzy silhouette, well beyond earshot of Gordon's angry obscenities.

When the bus conductor at last bothers to climb the stairs, somewhere north of King's Cross, he finds Gordon hunched over the rail of the seat in front. The conductor asks twice for the fare before shaking the passenger's very wet shoulder. Only then is there a pause between the snorts and sobs. As Gordon looks up, the conductor notes that the backs of the passenger's hands are patterned with tiny pools of tears, snot and rain.

☆

The world of Margaret Plimsoll is one reduced to images: continents of memories, their peaks echoing with half-remembered sounds, the valleys retaining smells that have lingered for years, and the shores dissolving into unlit wastes.
A will-o'-the-wisp of light punctuates the darkness. In one fraction of a milli-second, the light takes shape. A bonny young Highlander swings up from the shadowed valley. He is not just all sweet warmth but one particular afternoon.
Then he's gone. Gone with that July day. Absorbed in dove-grey cloud. Warm clouds, not chilly as slate or, even worse, the terrifying storm clouds on page one of Lady Ellen's Bible.
–*That is called an etching, Margaret.*
–*Why is this book covered in black? It frightens me like nightmares. . .*
–*All Bibles are black, Margaret. Life's not just threading daisies in a summer meadow. You're nearly thirteen now, you know. . .*
Gone. Warm gentle meadows of buttercups and daisies. Gone. And all warmth drained – all feeling, too – from these varicosed old legs. And the sounds, where have they gone? Is deafness this sudden? The haycart moves under the beeches, faltering up the lane, but why doesn't it creak? There's Prince, the golden labrador, opening his mouth but his bark is silent.
Stillness. The whole world still and dark. Nothing but a bedroom with the bedside candle guttered and out.
Nothing? Nothing at all?
Yes. A smell. Not the fresh scent of clover held under the nostrils. A pungent smell. Candle smoke in the terrifying dark? Not that. What then? . . . Disinfectant. That's it. The hospital smell. Can hardly be the delivery ward. Forty years too late for that. The recovery corridor, then, after the removal of that which was once fruitful? No. That must have been all of twenty years ago.
So where does the disinfectant lead? Is it the route, so often

trodden, through an empty corridor to that single bed in a side ward? March it was, though it should have been October. Outside, sown in the lawn, a golden host . . . a host of golden daffodils. Got it right. Not all the brain has peeled like an onion, even at eighty. Daffodils. But none next to John in that bed with the board already under his mattress for a journey to the mortuary. Poor John, a once attentive bridegroom, cancerous and yellow as an October leaf. Shrivelled and awaiting the final severance . . . But not this leaf. Some of us are not deciduous. No severing gale for Margaret yet awhile. Margaret MacCawdie's among the hardy perennials. . .

Very well . . . very well . . . Mrs Margaret Plimsoll, if you must fill out more forms. At least John's death was another severance. The last of that gushing Plimsoll gang. Life goes on. . .

More darkness? Could this be it? Impenetrable night, rushing higher than waves of that typhoon off the Madagascar coast? Hold on, Margaret. Hold firm. Don't dare to breathe and Mr Death the burglar may not spot you. Why are the clenched teeth soft as gums? Hold on. The labour ward was not the end. Neither may this be. . .

So, all over? Still breathing? That'll teach these young sprigs of doctors we Edwardians are tough.

A glimmer of light again? And a little warmth. Why shouldn't it come from the ten thousand tiny daisies in my private field?

Of course, all the waiting and the darkness were worthwhile. Here he comes: loping across the sloping grass, my bonny Alastair. More handsome every moment, my auburn cousin from his heathered island. With a lilt to his kilt on brawny thighs, Alastair swings nearer and so much clearer through the cloudless afternoon. There! He waves again, as he always did, with an arm like an oak mast.

He stands, protective as an oak, above his little cousin. Perhaps it should be a beech, with all that sun filtering through his Highland-coloured hair. No common little Lowlander, my Alastair. . .

–Mr Plimsoll? . . . Mrs Plimsoll? . . . Margaret? . . . Can you hear me?

Who's this damned nuisance, intruding on the daisy field?

–If you can't move your lips, Mrs Plimsoll, try fluttering your eyelids for me, will you, dear? . . . Take your time now, you're doing very nicely. . .

Flutter my eyelids? I'm no quayside whore. What's it all for? Pestering, always pestering. Forms to be signed . . . applications for a bus pass . . . supplementary pension books . . . When will it end? No sooner does a body get into a decent historical novel than it's the home help, or the district nurse or some damned interruption. . .

Flutter my eyelids, indeed! What does this one want? Come to let me know Little Beast has decided to favour his mother with a visit at long last? Here to ease his conscience, is he? Fat chance. Let him bring tributes from the Orient and marrons glacé from Harrods, it shall avail him nothing.

Tell him to go and play with himself. About all he's useful for. No woman'd want to play with him. What does he do with those men? What does he get up to with that string of nancy boys he brings for lunch? Only one decent fellow among them . . . too good for him, dirty Little Beast. . .

–No need to get restless, Mrs Plimsoll. You've nothing to worry about now. I'm your Night Sister. Have a good sleep now. There's no one to disturb you. We've got you a room all to yourself . . . I'll look in again in an hour. . .

A room to myself? What's the foolish girl blethering about? . . . Who's paying for it? Not Harry. Not Little Beast, that's for sure. Had John been alive, it would have been a different story. Nothing too good for Margaret then. Naturally a private room when Little Beast was born . . . What else, with all those hours on hours of appalling pain? . . . And for what? . . . A whining scrap of flesh from the moment they washed him down. At least I could look the neighbours, and those gushing Plimsolls, in the eye. But what else? . . . Cocksure little brat he became, thinking himself smarter than his parents. All those dreadful communist poems when he should have been out serving an apprenticeship. . .

And just where's it got you, Little Beast? . . . Writing bits of chatter about plays no decent-minded body would wish to see. Interviews with drug addicts and anarchists. Tea with a duchess, indeed. No time for a cuppa with me. I could have been found stone cold and rotting for all he cares.

How long was I by the phone before that Alastair-haired constable broke the window and found me? Wonder I didn't wet myself . . . All so sudden. One minute collecting an evening paper . . . the next, smack on the linoleum.

And how long before they found Little Beast? If they've found him yet, playing with one of his funny men in some public urinal. John was too gentle with him. Always thought the best of everyone. We both did. Never noticed our world was tumbling about like leaves on the common. All changed. Gone with those sailors drowned in the Kaiser's war.

–You're groaning again, Mrs Plimsoll. You've no pain now, have you, dear?

Why can't she go away? Sticking her mouth in my face. I can smell the chips even if her bog-Irish features are misty. I know an Irish brogue when I hear one.

–N-o-o-o.

–That's fine then, dear. You sleep now like a good girl. . .

Good riddance. She'll be much Harry's age. Not that they're all depraved like Little Beast. There's good and bad. That Alastair-haired constable for one. Could have done with John, all the same. Forty years leaning on his arm until it was brittle as a cherry twig. He'd hang cherries over my ears when we were courting. Better than the rice those vulgar Plimsolls showered us with. Lewd, the whole lot of them, with their suggestive jokes.

What was wrong with a cuddle before sleeping? Always enough for me. Just to know there was someone in the room, so one didn't need a candle. Who needs more? What pleasure was there in having that hairy lump of gristle pushed into me? All that grunting and sweating . . . Stains on John's pyjamas. Stains on my nice white sheets. Soon learned not to wash them straightaway. Fresh bed-linen seemed to rouse him. . .

–Mrs Plimsoll? I wouldn't be after disturbing you again but I was sure you'd be wanting to know Night Matron's just looked in at the door with your son. He wouldn't come in. . .

And I wouldn't want him. Does that shock you, my rosary-and-happy-families colleen? Why can't she hear me, instead of staring down like a moon with freckles? Let the Little Beast stay away from me. And you, too, Bridget the fidget. Stick to your bedpans and your breakfast trays. Make sure

you wash yor hands between the two. Just leave me, all of you.
Leave me to a little gardening, a decent romance from the library on wheels, and a spot of knitting for those less fortunate than myself. Yes, even for those blacks popping up everywhere nowadays. They've got to live somewhere. Not with me, of course. . .
Leave me, all of you, with my July days that the Kaiser and the doodlebugs tried to destroy. Didn't suceed, though. My daisy field's still intact . . . Not much else . . . Too many winters of slippery pavements and no sun from October to March. Insipid meals on wheels. And the long, freezing nights.
When will my limbs be warm again? Am I fated to be a stone figure on a chilly bed? Come back, July afternoons, come on back . . . Alastair, my strong and gentle cousin, when will you stride back into the meadow?

☆

The odds are against trouble, Harry's sure of it. Tricky moments during the past few years have been rare. It's a recollection that buoys his confidence as he fumbles for his door key. He feels – as he always hopes to be – in charge of the situation. All the same, wariness lingers round him like shadows in the ill-lit passage as he allows his visitor to pass. A five-minute chat under the dripping canopy of a coffee stall, followed by an exchange of monsyllables as they'd squelched through the sodden back streets of Waterloo, couldn't guarantee a trouble-free night. Not one hundred per cent. A stranger, Harry reminds himself, is a stranger is a stranger. His quarry's easy honesty might be just that. Equally, it could be a mask, fitting as snugly as his own.
–Need to move quietly. Some of 'em will be asleep.
The young man responds to Harry's whisper with a nod. Taking this as an acceptance of complicity, Harry does wish he could remember the name. Ted? Ed? Anyway, who the hell cared, in bed?
Doubts recur as he leads the way on tiptoe up the carpeted

stairs. Could that quick smile at the corners of the unworn lips be genuine or mechanical – the stock-in-trade of a street boy? It's unlikely, Harry reasons, that anyone in his early twenties would trot home with an older man without expecting to offer something in return for coffee and a chance to dry out in a warm bedroom.

Not a lot is said as Harry fills the kettle. His visitor rolls a cigarette. Both comment needlessly on gusts of wind that clout the window, spattering six months' grime with streaks of rain.

The fingers are stubby. Harry notes that, surmising that the nails have probably been broken through manual work rather than from nervous insecurities.

–Look . . . I'm sorry . . . you told me your name but. . .
–Forgot it already? Not surprising. Bet you don't remember a word I said back by the river. Over the hills and far away, you were, Harry. Name's Fred. . .
–Fred. Knew it was something like Ted or Ed.

They both laugh. Harry hopes his own eyes appear as uncalculating as those that look up at him. He can't be sure, since he's troubled by some mannerism of Fred's that puzzles him. Could it be the way laughter causes flesh round the eyes to crinkle? Harry let's the question go unanswered. He doesn't intend to drop his guard by romanticising a young man he's no expectations of seeing again.

The complexion and skin texture suggest Fred might be a country boy but Harry has long since given up the search for a flaxen-headed cowboy. With television discussions on the pros and cons of male relationships, and more outspoken magazines on the book stalls, even rustics from Perthshire and Penzance know the score.

–Glad you came along, Harry. Didn't fancy seeing the dawn in down there with the cider-freaks. . .

A simple statement, or the beginnings of a courtship dance? Since the kettle behind him is about to boil, Harry has a moment to deliberate this.

Just how much does any lad of say, twenty-three or thereabouts, know of one of London's oldest games? Ted or Ed, or even Fred, if that's his name, is of a generation impressed by Lionel Bart's musical, without ever having read a word of Dickens. Is Fred yet

one more who's cast himself as a waif-like Oliver, eager to be salvaged from the muddy riverside, happy to be bathed, scented and cuddled in a bower of lavender and muslin, relaxing in an overnight Eden until the harsher cries of the dole queue jerk him once more into a far from beautiful morning?
–Not from London, are you, Fred?
–The accent, you mean? Well, I've been around a bit, see? Go on, have a guess. . .
Without consulting Fred as to his preference for tea or coffee, Harry stirs coffee powder for them both, adds milk and pushes a mug across the formica table-top.
–Berkshire? Oxford way? Westish somewhere. . .
–Not bad, Professor Higgins. Been in Wiltshire for . . . quite a time. . .
Fred supplements the information with an open smile.
Just as he's about to pursue this, Harry becomes aware of an acrid stench. Since it's not the first time he's noticed it in the warmth of his kitchen, he knows the source well enough. Fred has neither showered nor washed his socks for two or three days at least.
–But now you're looking for gold on the London streets?
–Fat chance. A job'll do. Reckon I've got something fixed, too . . . Could be all settled in the morning. . .
With a practised touch, Harry flattens the tone of his voice and seeks a cliché. It's his democratic approach. No sensible fox, he reminds himself, approaches a chicken-run from upwind.
–What's your line of country, then?
–Most things, really. I'm adaptable, you might say. Stayed quite a while on the farm in Wiltshire. Pigs it was, mainly. When it got too nippy out on the hills I tried Manchester. Well, nearer Oldham. Cities are best in winter so I did a bit of window cleaning . . . Trouble was, it was always bloody raining. Did a few sessions posing at the local art school, too. Soon got pissed off with kids staring at my balls like I was a freak. Starts to knock your confidence, that does . . . Reckoned it was time to try London . . . Like I said, I'll get something. . .
–Even if it means the art schools again?
–No way. I'm a person, see? No one treats me like a bit of fresh meat; not Fred. . .

Remembering occasions on which he has been treated as such, Fred blushes. Harry, noting the colour rise, suffusing the cheeks to apple red, is hooked. Fred's compact build would have been enough. His curls, drying in the kitchen's warmth would have been a bonus. But the blush . . . Harry realises he's clenching the edge of the table. He's hooked. Any references by Fred to a girlfriend – even an estranged wife – will be no deterrent. An aphrodisiac, more like.

Time for Harry to reassert control of the situation.

–Better not talk too loud. The bloke in the next room to mine'll be back any minute. Works in a night club up West. . .

–Go on. What is he, bouncer or something?

–Right in one, Fred. Light-weight champion for somewhere years ago . . . so I heard. What's an ex-boxer to do for bread at forty-five? No problems though, if we're quiet. He's tame. So long as he gets his kip.

Not a flicker of amusement in Fred's eyes as Harry selects a down-market phrase. Instead he smothers a yawn.

–Thanks for coffee, Harry. Any chance I could stay over? Got a couch or anything?

–Wasn't thinking of pushing you out again. It's close on two. . .

–Thank Christ for that. Don't know where we are, anyway. Could be Timbuctoo High Street out there, for all I know. I'd just have to keep walking. . .

This observation – innocent enough – switches on amber warnings for Harry. Has he brought back someone homeless, a potentially clinging vine?

–Didn't you say something back at the coffee stall about it being a bit late to wake them up where you were staying?

–Well, yes and no. I'll be honest with you, Harry. I've lost my room by King's Cross. I mean, all I did was rinse a few socks and things in the hand-basin. Against their bloody rules, see? How was I to know they'd go in spying while I was out? But I'm not joining the homeless, not me . . . if that's what you're thinking. . .

–Who said what I'm thinking?

There's an edge in Harry's voice and he doesn't give a fart whether Fred hears it. Neither the younger man's background nor prospects interest him. Over-riding all else, for Harry, is his determination to get Fred between the sheets. Soon. It's reassuring that his visitor is not as tall as himself. He'd refute accusations of a wish to dominate while admitting that he likes to keep any new situation well in control.

–Can guess, though, can't I, Harry? Maybe you're thinking I was knocking round Charing Cross waiting for the first offer. If that was it, forget it. As it happens, I gave the brush-off to a couple of creeps before you strolled along. Another one as well, come to think of it, when I went for a piss in the station. . .

–Popular lad. . .

–No need to be sarkie. Want to know what this stupid berk said to me by the station toilet? . . . Some sort of student he was. I kid you not, Harry. Only wanted me to go back with him to discuss my sexuality. Can you credit it?

–You must admit the approach is different. . .

–Kinky, more like. Told him to bugger off and sort himself out. Would he listen? No. Pressed some bit of paper into my hand about meetings I should go to. . .

–And will you?

–What for? If I want a free tea and a bun, I'll make up a few sins for the Sally Army. Here, know what he said, this student? There's politics in sex . . . I ask you. Right, I said, work out the politics in this, mate. . .

–You hit him?

Although Harry does not welcome the prospect of violence, he's no longer scared by it. In selecting an overnight guest from the vast open-air warehouse of the riverside, he's only once made an error of judgement. Fortunately, glints of aggression became apparent in the kitchen rather than the bedroom. Harry was quite amazed at the haste with which the stranger, whose name he never learned, bolted down the stairs. A mere mention of the bouncer was sufficient.

–Hit him, Harry? . . . What for? . . . Felt sorry for him, in a way. Straight up, I did. Who's he conning, apart from himself? . . . No sense trying to hide a college accent under a load of theory, is there? . . . Never been into all this class bit myself . . . Me? I'm Fred, take it or leave it. No point in trying to guilt-trip me . . . Tell you what I reckon. Poor sod's running away from himself . . . Hit him? No need for it. Just gave him the old two fingers up

. . . Know what? . . . He shook his head at me like some injured vicar. Next minute he's starting on another bloke just coming up the toilet steps. . .

Harry lights a cigarette, glad that there's no immediate reason for ejecting Fred into the night.

Fred takes a first leisurely glance around the kitchen. He feels relaxed. The only comparison he can make is to evenings he'd enjoyed with his grandparents in Cranesview Terrace. He finds it hard to credit that the room in which he's sitting should be no more than a communal meeting point for strangers as they cook their meals. The walls and the woodwork could do with a freshening up but even the shabbiness seems to have character.

–Who else you got staying here then, Harry?

–Staying? Oh, you mean other tenants? . . . Well, there's a retired couple in the downstairs flat. He was a police sergeant. Mrs Duke was a teacher of sorts. More of a gymnast really. Not quite sure if it was weight-lifting or javelin. One of the two. . .

If the assortment of tenants seems odd to Fred, it in no way scares him. He supposes that there might be one or two policemen as gentle in their homes as they are aggressive in public. It could be that the bouncer, and the gymnast, are as interesting as Harry himself, under a tough surface. Whatever else he discovers in the next hour, Fred's sure the household isn't likely to include some of the kinky characters he's heard about, around the fires on waste lots where the homeless swop tales to while the night away.

There'll be no men who line their rooms with sheets of plastic and get their kicks from shitting on one another. On balance, he reckons it unlikely that the pensioners below the kitchen are diverting themselves with handcuffs filched from the local police station.

–Police? How do you cope with the law under the same roof?

–Nothing to cope with . . . It's quiet, cheap and walking distance to work. . .

The words flow so smoothly that Fred guesses they've been used often in similar circumstances. He still cannot pinpoint any good reason for Harry's agitation. It seems no big deal to Fred that, within minutes, the two of them will be snuggling close, exploring one another's bodies to offer and receive pleasure

until they are ready to sleep in friendly arms until morning. He concludes, without convincing himself, that Harry might have had some bad experiences before the law had been changed.
–We ought to make a move, Fred. . .
Even though the kitchen door is open, the stench from Fred's broken army surplus boots and socks is overpowering. Harry wonders, as he waits impatiently, if there might be – among the gay groups beginning to meet in every part of London – one patronised by those heavily into odours, stagnation and decay.
–Right then. Wouldn't want to get on the wrong side of the bouncer . . . Listen, Harry, any chance of a quick swill before we turn in?
–Why not?
With what he trusts will not be too obvious a hint, Harry throws a deodorant spray onto a towel he pulls from the bathroom cupboard. Fred dumps the spray without a glance and inspects the towel. It amuses Harry to think what the printed freize of Greek warriors in gold, brown and flame might convey to someone who has probably as much interest in the arts as he himself has in discos or football matches.
–Like this, Harry. It's great. These soldiers . . . all mates together, like.
–Just the first one to hand.
–I like it.
And I like him for all his off-hand manner, Fred thinks. I like him because he's wearing it like armour. Underneath he's as alone as I am. That's where I want to touch him. It's the inside of him, the part that's terrified of showing how warm it is, that I want holding me.
So Fred continues to examine the towel, at first with interest and then mechanically, it seems to Harry, as though playing for time. In a sense, Harry is right.
A worrying possibility has occured to Fred. Will Harry want to go the whole way – which is how Fred thinks of it – the first time? He's almost sure Harry won't pin him to the mattress and shove. Almost, but not quite. It's the recollection of his own first experience with a man that causes Fred to nip his lower lip between his teeth. As he stands in Harry's bathroom he is, for a moment, under a hedge beyond the pig-sties with Will

Chivers on top of him, grunting and thrusting, and not even having bothered to spit on those calloused hands.

And then he realises it is Harry standing close to him, offering a tube of toothpaste and a new brush.

–Thanks. All the gear's in a locker at the station. Must get it tomorrow. . .

Harry smiles wryly. If you get the job, he thinks, you'll ask for an advance. If you get that, you get your gear. If not, it's the downward spiral to join the dirty dozen under the arches at Charing Cross. . .

–Keep the brush, if you want.

–Thanks. Got a bucket anywhere?

–The shower's working. . .

–I meant for my socks. I'll soak them overnight. They pong like a pig-sty . . . Come on, admit it. . .

–Well, they're a bit ripe. Anyway, leave you to it. Don't make a mistake. It's up the next flight and then straight ahead.

Without waiting for Harry to leave, Fred pulls up his vest and singlet in one movement. His hair, now nearly dry, remains drawn up into a halo. An impulse to tear off his own clothes, lead Fred into the shower, to soap him and smother him with kisses, seizes Harry with such force that he turns abruptly and moves into the passageway.

–Won't keep you long, Harry. I mean, you've got to get some kip . . . We both have. . .

Fred shakes his head, grinning into the mirror on the back of the door, as he turns the key. There's little doubt in his mind that it will be he who has to make the first unambiguous move in what he supposes will be a double bed. From Harry, he's sure, there'll be nervous chatter till dawn unless it's halted by decisive action. The yawn and stretch that provide a reason for shifting one warm thigh against its eager neighbour will not be Harry's. When he's steeped his socks in a foam of soap powder and hot water, Fred turns his attention to his underpants. Inspecting skid marks along the seat, he regrets the curry he'd eaten twelve hours previously. A moment's hesitation and he plunges them in with the socks. It does occur to him that he'll have to walk naked through an unknown house in which a meeting with the bouncer can't be ruled out.

As he soaps himself, he considers the impression he might make on Harry. It's likely, he concludes, that a combination of muscles respectably toned and tanned by outdoor work, and the towel with its pattern of soldiers draped toga-fashion from one shoulder would prove a turn-on. He does hope Harry won't be spread naked and waiting on the bed-covers. If there's no adventure into the unknown then, for Fred, there's no fun. The only phrase he has ever remembered from the one Shakespeare play read at school is about love being a voyage of discovery. Discovery brings his thoughts full circle to the bouncer. If they should meet on the stairs, how could he explain his presence at half past two in the morning? Some distant cousin of Harry's? It's not until he's rinsing his pubic hair a second time to be sure he's got rid of crab lice that he chances on an answer that should put an ending to further questions. Fred has to bite his wrist to stop his laughter echoing through the silent house. He'll explain to the bouncer that Harry is his father.

☆

0245 hrs

Those words dear old Jack de Manio uses on his morning programme really fit the case: TGIF. Thank God It's Friday – and the end of another shift. What a dreadful way of looking at life – wishing the days away. If I go on like this, I'll soon be counting my shifts in hundreds, then tens, and I'll be sixty-five in no time. Is it mid-career blues? Professional menopause, as one of the psychologists said the other day? Rats to the causes. Main thing is to stop all this damned routine spilling over into my private life. How? The supermarket, launderette and returning library books have to be coped with as a priority. That, and a decent early night, sees the end of day one. A visit to Mother's has to be fitted in. So what's left? If the energy's there, a day return to see Sue, or a walk through Epping Forest. With weather like tonight's, even that's out. A bit of home-baking and an evening by the goggle-box. The soft option and I know it.
What else is a middle-aged woman supposed to do? Easier for a

man, e.g. Harry Plimsoll. All very fine for him to pretend he's not in his forties and go tearing around swinging London in a pair of jeans. With my hips I'd look like a bit of mutton dressed up as lamb.

Something has to be done about this crazy roster. It's Alice in Wonderland logic, really it is. The joys of being a Night Matron! All those days off you get, they say. And what's at the end of it all? Back to the slave pits to feel worse again. Would Sue's suggestion really work? What if I did chuck it in here and go private? My own boss at last? Lovely theory. Not hard to work out how it would be. Old hags oozing pearls and hypochondria using me as a skivvy day and night. Maybe it's better the devil you know. . .

Best of all though, might as well admit it, is Dimitri. Second best he may be but he's better than nowt, as old Sister Grice would have said. One more shift now, then it's up, up and away to that little white dot in the Aegean. Wonder if our trendy probationers ever suspect the secret life of Matron Humby? Bet they see me as over the hill. I'd be that, for them, at thirty-three, let alone forty-three. Overheard a couple in the corridor only last night whispering something about me giving myself in holy deadlock to the hospital. . .

Thanks to Dimitri, it's just not true. We'd a grim reminder enough against over-devotion to duty earlier this month. Dear old Sister Grice. Thirty-five years' service and the last ten planning a round the world trip for her retirement. Well, at least she did it before she keeled over in the tube home. Not much of a home to come back to, poor soul. A bedsit in Peckham with a window-box and a one-eyed cat.

That has to be avoided. Question is: how? Something to be thought about. Soon. How long, for instance, can Dimitri and I go on? Ten years isn't a bad record. Nine years more than I had with the bloody mountie with the bounty. How long, then? Best to play that one as it goes, from visit to visit.

Does it matter if the whole thing started as a cliché? Falling for a tour guide's better than signing up with a marriage agency any day. At least D and I didn't meet in some cafeteria and have to size one another up over plastic food.

Does his wife know? Not that it matters. And does it really

matter who pays for the car hire? What's important is waking up beside someone you like. How it would work out on a day-in-day-out basis is another matter. We both know that.

Say it did end, not this time, but in September, sometime between the fifth and sixteenth? If it did, one thing's certain. I'd not bother to look for anyone else. After all, what's a diary for if one can't be honest?

Guess Mother suspects about Dimitri. Never to worry. She doesn't grudge other people a bit of happiness. Don't think Ricky would either. We've never been a demanding family. Not like old Margaret Plimsoll. She'll have us all dancing round her once she's sitting up and taking nourishment.

It really has been the coincidence of all time. Two — not one — two figures from the past turning up when least expected. Harry Plimsoll still fettered to the old harridan after a quarter of a century. He didn't seem a total stranger. Some things about him haven't altered. Can't wait to tell Sue. Could send her a letter rather than a card from Greece. She was right all those years ago. Would have been madness to have encouraged him. A worse catastrophe than the mountie.

Must probe a little deeper when he drops in for a drink. There's something sad about him. No, not sad — unfulfilled. Still seems to be fighting for some ideal world instead of getting on with things as they are. Must ask if he still writes poems. More intriguing, who has he got hidden away? One, or more than one. . . ?

We'll have trouble with him in the weeks ahead. I know the signs. Don't envy the Almoner, having to cope with Mother Plimsoll's future. Harry will scream long and loud. Not that he'll be the first or last. Poor old Harry. There are penalties in being an only child born late in life. Damned sight more so if he'd been a girl.

0315 hrs. Another round in a few minutes. The rain appears to be easing so maybe there'll not be another soaking at the bus stop.

Will there be a card from Ricky on the mat? Where from this time? Ireland again? Maybe somewhere else to add to my collection: Dundee, Salisbury, Brecon. It's like following a travelling circus.

Will he ever settle so we can all have a good laugh about his wanderings? If he'd only give a hint now and again about how he actually earns his bread. I believe him when he says he'd never take the dole. But what does he do? Like his grandfather in that as well – ready to turn his hand to most things?

At least he rings Mother once a month and pops in between changing trains or buses. Knows he won't be pressed for details by her. I try not to. Not again, after last time. Let's hope he'll risk another face-to-face with me sometime soon.

Another sign of middle age that I think about him more in weather like this? I really must accept that he's a grown man. In Greece he'd have been married and a father by now, as D pointed out. But who am I to encourage anyone into marriage? Let's not grudge him the independence I never had at his age.

All the same, let's hope he doesn't join one of these hippy communes. I've seen where innocent experiments with drugs end up. It's some comfort to know he's inherited the family common sense. Trouble is, he's becoming more and more private. Like Dad again, unwilling to have his feelings hurt. Well, we gave him as good a grounding as we could. He got more affection than old Margaret Plimsoll ever offered anyone except herself. . .

Damn. That's two ambulances by the sound of it. Casualty, here we come. The early hours dust-up at Waterloo Station, I'll bet my pension. . .

☆

Gliding his fingertips over firm belly muscles, it occurs to Harry that he might take up the piano again. He debates this silently, continuing to stroke the hairless abdomen, until he chances on one of Fred's erotically vulnerable spots. A gasp of pleasure disturbs Harry's plan for an expedition among the second-hand shops of Walworth Road, and he concentrates a little more on the body alongside him. He searches for an appendix scar. Finding none, he's irritated rather than disappointed. Fred's body is too perfect. He recollects, as a comparison, the dark scars left on Gordon's stomach by an ulcer operation. Such defects have always been a comfort. Imperfections make Harry less conscious of his own flaccid biceps and his penis that seems so boyish until roused. So he's never been disappointed by those who've brought to his bed stringy thighs, shoulders fleeced with hair, or balls no bigger than a pair of garden peas. Fred is an irritant, summoning up images of Harry's long-forgotten teens and his first two lovers. In short, he threatens Harry's orderly routine of taking a well-earned sedative after a taxing day.

Harry's fingers drift lightly up to check whether the soft nipples have now hardened. Another triumph. With thumb and finger he tests the ripeness of two small berries. The torso arches and Fred's hand gropes in a hungry, but not practised way, on Harry's shoulder blades. When Fred's chin, more furred than stubbled, seeks Harry's neck, there's a waft of something other than bath soap and toothpaste. He's beginning to sweat with excitement. For Harry, it's a natural amyl nitrate. What's more, it costs no more than a little effort.

Light as a pebble skimming the wave-tops, Harry moves his fingers down Fred's body once more. He observes the effect with interest, and surmises that Fred's experiences might be limited to schoolboy fumblings or the let's-get-it-up-and-over-with amateurs to be found in suburban parks. He's certainly catching his breath, waiting for a hand other than his own to light on his groin.

But Fred is temporarily disappointed. Quite ready to enjoy a couple of climaxes before they sleep and then another at dawn, while sparrows chatter in trees along the street, it doesn't cross his mind that Harry might not feel the same. Neither can he know the urgency of Harry's secret need to be fondled equally, hugged with more than pretended warmth, and brought to more than routine orgasm.

Nor does Fred hear Big Ben striking three. Harry does, and considers how much longer he should prolong Fred's pleasure. He's already anticipating a last, post-coital cigarette before turning his face from Fred and relaxing into his own private dream.

Interested to discover how far Fred can be excited before reaching an involuntary climax, Harry thrusts his face between

parted thighs. His foraging tongue grows salty and, as he nuzzles deeper, his lips touch hair soft as the first croppings of spring grass. He senses Fred's delight, and hopes that within minutes he might be eager to do likewise. If Fred hesitates, Harry considers reminding him that Francis of Assisi scooped lepers' spittle from the gutters and placed it on his tongue. Doubts as to whether the comparison is apt are interrupted.
–Christ, Harry . . .
–Uh?
–Shit, I never knew it could be as mind-blowing as this . . .
–Glad you're enjoying it . . .
–And you?
–What d'you think?
Since Harry's raised his head momentarily, Fred can ruffle his hair. Harry makes use of the pause to check his watch. They have been in bed thirty-six minutes. He resolves to set the alarm for a quarter to eight. With Fred gone by a quarter past, it should be possible to take a shower and be back in bed for another few hours before facing the afternoon.
Meanwhile? . . . Action.
Judging from the quick cry of ecstasy, there's reason to suppose that Fred's delighted by the sudden directness of Harry's love making. Harry's lips rest on the tip of Fred's cock before they open to allow his tongue make a gradual circuit. The shape reminds Harry of a fully-grown strawberry. They should be, he calculates, on the market stalls within six weeks. He does concede they will be no more satisfying than the sweet, plump fruit that's throbbing in his mouth. For Harry, the question is not whether the fruit would as delicious a second time but what increased price would he have to pay. As his lips move down and ease back with a steady rhythm, he's very tempted to incorporate Fred in his roster on a once a week basis. It would solve the problem of Docklands Bob, who's becoming keener every visit. Or Fred could replace Gordon. This might be even more satisfactory. Bob's little presents that had tumbled from the back of a truck have never posed any real challenge. Gordon, however, weighed down by the luggage of a life-long affair spells trouble. No matter how he denies it, Harry is certain that Gordon would lead him towards a repugnant domesticity:

dinner ready at eight on the dot and tantrums if the soup has cooled.
—Not yet, Harry. Hold it, mate. Hold it. I'll come if you don't ease up. . .
Still thinking of Gordon, Harry does comply. If Fred hears a crack from Harry's ankle joints, he doesn't comment on it. He folds his arms round Harry and, after their third kiss, moves so that, cheek-bone to cheek-bone, he can whisper into the shadows that have no disapproving eyes.
—Want me to turn over for you?
Turning Fred's face towards him, Harry frames the jaw between his palms. Fred's eyes are warmer than the street-lamp's glow but his teeth are sunk so far into his lower lip that Harry guesses they must be trembling. It's clear that Fred wants to offer all but is scared.
Quite unbidden, a secret terror confronts Harry. Would Fred expect a similar offer? It's not often that such a response has been expected of Harry but it has happened. He checks over the colourful refusals he's made in the past: having been raped as a choirboy has led to a psychological block, suffering from anal warts would make it painful, my piles are bad tonight . . .
—Do you, Harry?
—Not this time . . . No . . . relax . . .
Fred's kiss is the warmest yet. It relaxes Harry and opens his mind to another possibility. After all, on balance, it would be best not to see Fred again. The age difference would limit topics in common and, different though their backgrounds might be, Harry is growing bored with culling information from his pick-ups to provide notes for yet another article on London's disadvantaged. He really would prefer to move on to political analysis and travel features.
Putting himself in Fred's place, just for an instant, Harry feels it's improbable that any twenty-three-year-old wanderer will want to make much of a one-night stand.
—Ever go to any of the gay bars, Fred?
—What a question. I mean, at a time like this. Why?
—Just wondered how well you knew London . . .
—Know where they are. So what're they going to offer when there's decent blokes I can find for myself . . .

–Like me?

Harry waits. Will there be some declaration that sets the alarms going? Fred laughs quietly in the darkness, refuses an explanation and runs his tongue across Harry's eyelids.

No one has ever done this before to Harry. He drops back onto the pillow and lies with his eyes closed. Enjoying the sensation of tongue-tip brushing his nose, chin and neck like a feather, he transforms Fred into an unexpected demi-god who's flown in – a bit bedraggled from the rain – to possess and gratify in the darkness. Fred is a youthful deity who will vanish before dawn glints on his ethereal feathers. He is the silent partner in a secret act, to be remembered but never encountered again. Harry opens himself to an enfolding and dominant stranger, though the dominance will be one that is limited to gratifying his private needs.

With a swift heave, he pulls Fred over to cover him. There's a tiny sound as Harry fills his palm with spittle and coats the inner reaches of his crotch. Fred needs no guidance, and Harry, controlling a sigh, feels the first sure plunge and clamps his thighs under Fred's own. Catching and matching each other's rhythm, they close and part, offer and receive. The dance is not long, curtailed by Fred's abstinence and Harry's seldom-admitted need. Soon enough, Fred gasps, thrusts more quickly and then drops into the crook of Harry's neck.

Dabbing the nut-brown hair with his lips, Harry lifts an arm to squint at his wrist-watch. It occurs to him that it's early closing day at the launderette so he'll be unable to enjoy as long a lie-in as he'd anticipated. His annoyance is lost in amazement as he becomes aware of his own unsatisfied erection. About to mention this to Fred, and suggest something needs to be done, Harry hears a deep, contented snore.

☆

Rain washes the slates and pavements of South London as it has done, almost without a pause, for ten days and nights. It forms pools of mud among the gardens of the Imperial War

Museum, and clearer pools in the awnings over market stalls along Lower Marsh. Falling on the Thames, it does nothing to brighten the sour grey water flowing under Westminster Bridge. In a negative way, it brings some almost selfish comfort to the patients and staff of the hospital. Unlike office workers, the few early tourists, the homeless and the shoppers, they are insulated from discomfort by the concrete slabs and plate-glass windows of a tower block.

In a corner room on the seventh floor, Margaret Plimsoll draws a crocheted shawl round her throat, pulls a scarlet blanket further into her lap and studies the view. It calls to mind for her a French painting reproduced on a calendar she'd once been given. She fails to recall the donor while remaining certain it was a New Year's gift. The picture itself she recollects more clearly. There had been a woman in a ground-length blue dress such as Margaret's mother had worn. The artist had given his model a bonnet to match. Was there an umbrella, too? Margaret lets that pass, though she's sure it had been raining in Paris at the time. Paris had been prominent in the game that she'd played with John when he was clearly dying. They'd both pretended they would visit France when he recovered. She tries again to think who might have given her the calendar. It could have been sherry-sodden Winnie, babbling about it being a suitable gift for the artistic one of the family. Or it might have been Harry, the Little Beast, bearing a cheap peace-offering after a row.

Margaret tires of speculation. Only the image of herself hanging the calendar above her downstairs toilet remains.

Reaching for a glass of orange juice, she sips from it while counting tourists stepping out of a coach on Westminster Bridge. Luxuriating in her own comfort, she spares a thought for them as they huddle under umbrellas. Holidaying in London in March, she thinks, is a poor second best when compared with vacations she once enjoyed in Kenya. The planting rains in the Ngong Hills had been sharper but predictable and brief. One day the slopes would be as dry as yellowed bones. After an all-night torrential downpour, the view from the verandah would be transformed. There'd be buds on the frangipani and a tapestry of rock plants.

She recalls the Kenyan landscape as beautiful in a harsh, almost

violent way, one that could never rival the softer slopes of Hertfordshire with its fields of buttercups and daisies. When she said as much to John and Alastair they laughed. Alastair's more rounded, confident laugh echoes still after more than forty years. As Margaret tries to recapture that morning, she emits a long sigh. She replaces the fruit juice on a wheeled table and addresses the window.
–Who's left to laugh with me now?
In answer to this, another strange face, surrounded with ringlets elongated by the rain, appears in front of her. Unsure who it might be, Margaret assumes the kindliest of smiles.
–And what can I do for you, dear?
–Did no one tell you I'd be popping in for an hour this afternoon, Mrs Plimsoll?
–I don't think so. But this room's like a parade ground. It never stops. You'd think I was royalty. . .
Amanda hopes the old bird won't prove to be impossibly gaga. Only the previous week there'd been a disaster. The interview with a distinguished singer that she'd so counted on as the centrepiece of her research had just fallen apart. The old dear of eighty-plus had mixed up operas and pantomimes – even the titles. Amanda had just given up when the former diva wept for twenty minutes about her canary that had been killed in an air raid.
–Well, Mrs Plimsoll, I hope I'm not going to be a nuisance. Night Matron Humby arranged it. That's to say, she thought you might like to talk to me. I expect you remember her from years ago. .
–Humby? Now wasn't that my cleaning woman during the war? I used to let her have our margarine ration and we'd buy her butter. She'd been brought up on the stuff, you see. We hadn't . . . I know Dr Summerskill swore no one could tell the difference, but then Edith Summerskill was a socialist. . .
While she's speaking, Margaret studies the young woman who's hanging a damp grey duffel coat behind the door. Why, she wonders, does everyone want to wear drab colours? The only answer she's ever been able to come up with is that Harry's generation seems intent on appearing like a collection of monks and nuns ready to serve some cause or other.

It crosses Margaret's mind that her visitor could be a psychologist preparing some cunning memory test that will decide whether the future is to be a place in a home for geriatrics.
–No, Mrs Plimsoll. Not your cleaning woman. Night Matron Humby was your son's girlfriend. She started as a student nurse just as he was going to college. Noreen Humby. . .
Instantly wary at the mention of Harry, Margaret feels it's prudent to play for time. The gates of a home for the elderly take firmer shape, together with a query that has never been answered to her satisfaction. Are inmates allowed to keep their own clothes or must they wear the uniforms provided? Harry has accused her of self-dramatisation but Margaret isn't convinced. Having read *The Daily Telegraph* for more than two decades she's never found a report that the regulations had been changed. What proof then, that conditions had altered since Charles Dickens and Thomas Hardy described what they'd seen with their own eyes?
It's best, she decides, to choose her words with extra care.
–A girlfriend? When you've a grown son of your own, dear, you'll get used to girlfriends popping in and out all the time. Now, when my Harry's really settled in his career, able to offer a wife something, if you know what I mean, that'll be the time to talk of marriage. . .
With her tape recorder settled on the parquet floor, Amanda Sopworth goes to the window to fetch an upright chair. Margaret's words puzzle her and she recalls what she can of the notes she's scanned hastily in the lift. Harry, or whatever his name is, just has to be forty. It seems odd that Margaret should refer to him as though he were barely out of college.
But Margaret is staring at the tape recorder, trying to decide whether it could be some new gadget that will measure her heart-beat or how well her newly implanted pacemaker is behaving.
–Yes, I'm sure you're right, Mrs Plimsoll. It's you I'd like us to talk about, though. . .
A protest, perhaps on the lines of being far happier in her own company than answering more questions, surfaces in Margaret's mind. True enough, she would prefer to glance through a magazine until a supper that includes underdone steak, not

more steamed fish, arrives on a nicely laid tray. To voice such a protest could be hazardous. She knows that. One could live to regret any criticism of the hospital's system.

–Me, dear? What's there to talk about? I'm a bit of wreckage washed up on the tide . . . It's all yesterdays for me, nowadays. What's so interesting in that?

–You've gone straight to the point, Mrs Plimsoll. It's your yesterdays that are the fascinating things for me. You've travelled . . . met unusual people. . .

–My dear son, Harry, says people are only interested in a new future . . . What's your name, dear?

–Amanda. I see yours is Margaret . . . May I call you that?

Margaret stares at a woman almost young enough to be a grand-daughter – a relative she's never likely to have. A sudden smile reunifies her broken features. She remembers one home help's attempt at intimacy and her own polar response. That had put the saucy little baggage in her place. No *Margaret dearie* after that.

–If you wish, Amaryllis. . .

–Amanda.

–A pretty name. Names should always be derived from flowers. Such a pity they reserve Buttercup for cows . . . and Daisy for cockney charwomen.

–That's something I'd never thought of, Margaret . . . Well, now . . . I'm working on a thesis. I wonder if you know what that is?

–I've always been a reader, dear. I sometimes think my son might be working secretly on a thesis. Harry takes such an interest in London's homeless, you know. These young men who've served in the army and navy, mainly. So many seem quite lost as to what to do with their evenings when they've been demobbed. Harry counsels them, I think that's the word. It wouldn't surprise me if he was putting all his experiences with them into a thesis. . .

As Amanda plugs in the microphone, she does wonder about Harry Plimsoll's motivation. Could it be a myth, invented to explain absences from the old chatter-box? Or maybe the usual story of the middle-class intellectual assuaging his guilt?

–That's really fascinating, Margaret.

–I'd not have the patience. I've seen some of them at the street corners myself. The smell from some of them, Amaryllis, you'd not credit it. One would think there were no public bath-houses left. . .

–My husband's doing a television series on London's homeless. Wouldn't it be a coincidence if he and your Harry had met? Jeremy's research takes him out at odd hours. Sometimes he's away half the night in his tracksuit. If he didn't wear that, none of them would talk to him, you see . . . Well, we mustn't digress, must we? . . . My work's much nicer. Talking to interesting people like you with their own stories to tell. It's what we call oral history. . .

–How very odd. History used to be about kings and queens . . . and battles. Princes, as well. Some from Scotland. So all that's changed now, has it?

Still not sure if she's chanced on another rambler, Amanda tests the microphone with a scratch or so. It registers on the volume meter so all seems to be well.

–Who do you think wrote that old kind of history, Margaret?

–Well . . . gentlemen from Oxford, I should suppose. We'd hoped at one time Harry would go there. Between ourselves, he was a bit of a flibberty-gibbet when he was young. Took after his father's side of the family. And a red hot socialist he was, too. . .

–Fascinating. Well, Margaret, I'm sure your son would agree it's not just kings and battles we should think of. There's another world that gentlemen from private schools never seemed to notice. . .

–You sound like Harry. Not from *The Daily Worker*, are you?

–Heavens, no. I'm a sociologist. . .

–Well, I suppose that's different. Let me tell you, Amaryllis, there's nothing wrong with gentlemen. I've met some very cultured men in my time. In Nairobi, of course. The less fortunate went to Rhodesia . . . And after we came home, as well . . . Look at me now, a bag of old bones tied in the middle. Wouldn't think I'd had tea in Downing Street, would you?

Amanda is reassailed by doubts. Is she about to hear a reminiscence or some wish-fulfilment? The latter's always a possibility since people of Margaret's age have few contemporaries to contradict them. It's best, she feels, to go along with the old woman, since it's feasible that someone now living in Cosmo Gardens, Vauxhall, might have seen more glittering afternoons than those spent in a bingo hall or a day centre.

–Fascinating. Do you mind if I turn on this tape recorder?
–Are we going out live, dear? Is this the Jack de Manio programme?
–Would that it were. They'd pay me better. . .
–You get paid to do this?
–Well, there's a grant that keeps body and soul together, Margaret. . .
–It's the war all over again. Decent young married women like you working machines. Poor Amaryllis. . .
–Amanda.
–That's a pretty name, too. Well, dear, where do you want me to begin? . . . I was born in the closing years of the last century . . . that sort of thing?
–That could come later. How about your visit to Downing Street? Who was there?
–It was all so long ago. I can't remember half of them. General Smuts was, that I do know. Odd to meet him after all those years. . .
–You'd known him in childhood?
–Not at all, dear. He wasn't on our side, was he? Not then. You know, I told him my very first memory was being pushed down the hill in the post cart between fields of clover. The postman pushed me. We were on the way to our market town, you see. I held a tiny flag in my hand, and I joined in with the village children as we all sang. . .
–What did you sing?
–Well, *One, Two, Three, Relief of Kimberley*, of course.
–And what did General Smuts say to that, Margaret?
–He laughed. Yes, I'm sure he did. A very upright gentleman he was. . .
–But on the side of the Boers?
–A detail, dear. Wars never divide the gentry. Anyone who's anyone in Europe's related. Take the last war. This present queen's sisters-in-law. . .

–Let's not stray too far, Margaret. What about Downing Street? You actually met Mrs Churchill there?
–You're confusing me, dear. One question at a time. The only occasion on which I met Mrs Churchill was at the Dorchester Hotel. She was going into the gentlemen's lavatory at the time. Very preoccupied she must have been . . . Of course, those children of hers were a handful, and no mistake. Parenthood's never an unmixed blessing, is it? Do you have children of your own?
–No, Margaret. Perhaps one day . . . So, who else did you meet in Downing Street?
–Well, there was that funny little body Clem Attlee married, of course. She just poured Indian tea for me without even asking if I'd prefer a cup of China.
Amanda checks that the recorder's take-up spool is not fouling. Noting that all is well, she feels free to hold the conversation on course.
–What was the real reason for the tea party?
–Oh, some charity or other. My brother-in-law was always giving donations. He was our mayor, you know. Harry could have come, too. He hated what he called all our bourgeois nonsense. Always reading Shaw at the time. John, my husband, was really worried that Harry might be hanged for his socialist ideas. Dreadful business, hanging. I was always told they wet themselves with terror on the scaffold. Or worse. Do you think it's true?
–Well, it doesn't matter now, Margaret. They don't hang people any more. . .
–More's the pity. All this mugging and gangs roaming the streets every weekend. They'll be squatting in Fortnums next. . .
–I don't think that's likely . . . Tell me, Margaret, am I tiring you? I did promise the ward sister. . .
–Nonsense, dear. It's always good to talk if you've got a sympathetic listener. I'm quite amazed my Harry isn't here. A devoted son, if ever there was one. Always busy though . . . these men. . .
–Could we have a little more about your childhood? I mean, after the Boer War. .? Do you mind going back over it? I find all that really fascinating.

–There are times when I wish I could go back and stay there. All those hillsides in flower . . . Well dear, my upbringing was a little different from most. There was a shadow on my lung when I was a toddler. Not TB you understand. That was common enough among the poorer children. All I had was a shadow. So I was put in the care of a maiden lady . . . Lady Ellen. She had a dower house near Watford. Now she was a lady born, Amaryllis, the daughter of an earl, not some jumped-up knight's wife . . . We'd maids to attend to our daily wants, naturally. Six, I seem to remember. And six of us . . . And we had a qualified nurse on the staff . . . Would you be a kind girl and pass my orange juice?

Doing so with a mechanical gesture, Amanda wonders if Margaret increasingly prefers this idyllic past to the present. It wouldn't be surprising. She also questions whether there's some ambiguity in the old woman's relationship with her son. Something seems amiss, but Amanda concedes she might be over-sensitive about relationships as a result of growing doubts concerning her own marriage.

–Now, dear, where were we?

–In Hertfordshire. So, how old were you then, Margaret?

–Didn't I say? How odd. I was five. Stayed there until I was thirteen. On my thirteenth birthday my cousin Alastair travelled all the way from Scotland to be with me. It was a perfect July day. Not one cloud in the sky. The last day I ever remember like that . . . Afterwards, everything began to change. I'd have been terrified if we hadn't had a nurse. . .

–Terrified of something Alastair had. . . ?

–What can you be thinking of? There was nothing like that when I was a child . . . Not among the people we mixed with. No . . . I meant, dear, that I started to grow up . . . just as all girls do at thirteen or thereabouts. . .

Amanda conceals a smile.

–How stupid of me. You mean you had your first period?

–Your generation is so much more outspoken. Everything's on television now. All the mystery's gone though, hasn't it? . . . All you young people hopping into one another's beds before marriage . . . Not just men and women either, from what I read. I find it sad. I really do, Amaryllis. What's left to be discovered after the wedding bells? . . . There's no time for romance nowadays, is there?

–Well, my husband and I didn't live together before we went to the registry office, if that cheers you up. Anyway, tell me about your first romance, Margaret.

Directly she's spoken, Amanda leans down in a panic. The recording level seems to be dropping for no logical reason. She raps the glass protecting the volume meter with irritation. As inexplicably as it has faltered, it revives.

Only half-aware that Margaret is not as forthcoming with an answer as she has been throughout their conversation, Amanda supposes the lively old eyes have misted over at some memory. When she does raise her head to offer an encouraging smile, she's met with a black stare, as though she's committed some gaffe far graver than the reference to menstruation. Margaret's fingers are gathering and regathering the hem of her blanket into endless pleats.

–First romance? Whatever can you mean? I must say, you do have the strangest ideas. There was only one romance. . .

–How fascinating, Margaret. It was love at first sight then? I suppose it was easier for your generation . . . I mean, no television or film heroes to send you off searching for. . .

–Nonsense, dear. We'd picture books, hadn't we? Burne-Jones and Lord Leighton . . . And there were novels. Not, of course, the smutty ravings of D.H.Lawrence. I read that dreadful book later on. It was passed round at the club in Nairobi. Wrapped in brown paper, of course. . .

–Of course. Now, back to something far more pleasant. Your first love. It was John, your husband?

For a moment, Margaret considers the rain – which seems to be easing – in silence. Indeed, she spots a smudge of watery blue above Big Ben.

–And who else should it have been, Amaryllis? Ordinary people weren't encouraged to be flighty when I was a girl. There were stories about those in the very highest reaches of society, I'm not denying that. You know the one about Queen Mary? . . . Well, I'll tell you. It was said that princess or not, she'd allowed herself to be carried away – that's how we put it – carried away by King George's elder brother. She'd been engaged to him first, you understand . . . Anyway, he died and she had to marry old strait-laced George pronto. Now this is the point. The wedding came only after she'd gone on a six-month cruise to Malta. To get over her grief, so it was said. There was many a Portsmouth sailor could have told you she was so upset she never came on deck once . . . on the way out. After a few weeks in Malta it was all public appearances again . . . Now, you can make what you like out of that. . .

–Fascinating. Well, even princesses are human, Margaret. But you were never tempted?

–Do you know, dear, I suddenly feel quite exhausted with all this chattering. Perhaps we could go on some other time? . . . When you're my age, the energy's limited . . . Would you be a kind girl and push the bell? . . . I haven't even the energy to lean that far. Since we're speaking frankly, Amaryllis, I think I need to use the bedpan. And then I'm going to take a little nap before supper.

Increasingly unsure of just how far she's been playing audience to a brilliantly manipulative actress, Amanda Sopworth turns off her tape recorder and stands up. She's determined not to be fobbed off without arranging a second session.

–That's really super, Margaret. I'd love to come again, you know. We've done so splendidly this time I didn't notice how the minutes were ticking on. Next week we could start with when you and John first. . .

–Yes, dear . . . Yes. Do ring that bell, will you? I don't think I can hold it much longer. . .

☆

–What the fuck are you doing here?

It's not been an afternoon when Harry's felt he's had everything going for him. To have returned to the editorial offices after a few days, when he's not been expected for a month, hasn't provoked the relief and delight for which he's been hoping. There's been no offer of immediate shift work. No pointing him towards a typewriter with explanations that some colleague has scratched a retina with his contact lens, and another has attempted to embarrass her chauvinist boss with pleas that her coil has slipped.

The casual disinterest with which he's been greeted in corridors has grazed his insecurities. In less than an hour, he's even suspecting they might be edging him towards the end of the plank.

Why then should he have chosen to fill part of an afternoon by going there at all? He dislikes the answer more than the question. Anything: the launderette, second-hand piano shops, a Fleet Street bar, are all welcome diversions that can keep him moving, instead of sitting biting his nails to the quick. He's even considered, more than once, taking his air ticket – together with a bogus letter and a forged signature – to Heathrow, and explaining that his failure to report for the Sydney flight was as a result of having to cover a bomb scare.

To leave the building, and come face to face with Gordon Laird in the alleyway leading to Fleet Street itself is that last straw which he does not intend to suffer willingly.

–I said, What the fuck are you doing here?

–Happened to be passing, Harry. Just sheltering under the arch until this shower eases.

Gordon doesn't expect to be believed. For some days he's debated how far he's lowering his pride by even thinking of tracking Harry. Recalling that Blair had always said pride didn't come into it when there was true affection, Gordon has taken a day off work and spent the morning among magazines in his local reference library. A couple of signed articles and a confirmatory phone call have brought him to the alleyway. Information volunteered by the switchboard that Mr Plimsoll is on holiday in Australia puzzled Gordon until his fingers touched a scrap of paper with a non-existent phone number scrawled on it. A pattern begins to take shape. The switchboard operator has been bribed to cover the tracks of Harry Plimsoll, the trickster.

–Happened to be passing? What a coincidence, Gordon. A few more minutes and you'd have missed me. Shame. I'm on my way to the hospital.

Gordon is instantly all concern.

–Nothing serious, Harry?

–Nothing for you to fantasise about. You won't need to sit wiping my fevered brow until I wake to know you've always loved me for my shy and generous self. Forget that little number, mate. . .

–What the hell are you on about, Harry? . . . Someone in there been giving you a hard time? . . . I told you, I just happened to be passing. . .

–Just happened to be passing wind, darling. Can't you do better than that?

–I can, too. I thought we'd a date some evenings back at the Hermes Tavern. You stood me up, and I've had never a word in explanation. The least you might have done was phone. And what's all this cover story, with them thinking back there you're in Australia?

–Checking up on me at work now, is it?

–I was worried you might be ill. I see you're not. What's the hospital bit? Another game? . . . How many other Gordons have you got in tow, eh?

Although Gordon's anger is fairly well controlled, he's not bothered to lower his voice since the alleyway seems deserted. Harry, with his back to Fleet Street, spots a couple of his colleagues nipping out for an early evening beer, and thinks it best to move Gordon out of earshot. More privately, Harry hasn't expected such a spirited argument and feels at a disadvantage. He starts to put up his umbrella.

–All right, Gordon. All right then. I owe you a bit of an explanation . . . Got half an hour? I honestly am on my way to the hospital . . . In a way it's connected with Australia. Everything's such a mess . . . Want to hear about it over a drink?

There's the slightest of pauses before Gordon accepts. He's confused. In part, already feeling guilty that he's attacked without considering whether there might be honest reasons for Harry's seemingly callous behaviour, he still needs to keep firmly in mind the possibility of more half-truths and inconsistencies. Hopes that the two of them – much of an age, and undoubtedly attracted physically to each other – can find a way of building something together are still strong in Gordon. All he can offer is empathy. He sees Harry as an animal, cornered by circumstance, that will spit and claw unpredictably but a creature that must respond finally to kindness and understanding.

–I'd rather have a coffee or some tea. Look, the rain's easing. Why don't we try that restaurant in the park along the Embankment?

–Opposite the all-night coffee stall? Christ, Gordon, is there no end to your nostalgia? . . . Where first we met . . . an old song from the Land of the Loch and Heather, and here to sing it is your own, your very own. . .

–Give it a rest, will you, Harry? It's half-way to the hospital. I was thinking of you. . .

–Then bloody well stop thinking of me, will you?

–Perhaps I should. You seem to think little enough of others. . .

–All right. All right, Gordon. I'm under pressure at the moment. Coffee is it?

As they manoeuvre between the puddles and flooded gutters of a side street leading to the Victoria Embankment, frail sunlight breaks from among the clouds at last. Commuters, wan-faced as the sun itself, furl their umbrellas. They scurry on, over-taking Gordon and Harry, then reconverging in front of them like soldier ants who've been interrupted in a march between their offices and Charing Cross Station.

At the restaurant in the park some member of staff has had the forethought to stack the white plastic garden chairs during the latest downpour. Gordon and Harry lift a couple and carry them to a nearby table that's clear of the dripping plane trees. There's an instant warning, from the interior of the café, that the place will be closing in fifteen minutes. Could the cafés of Sydney or Melbourne be less welcoming, Harry wonders as he carries two thick cups, overfilled with a caramel-coloured liquid, to the slopping wet table? With an ungracious wave, a hand at the cash desk offers a towel so that Gordon can mop up the worst of the smutted pool.

–Look, Gordon. Believe this or not, just as you wish. I'd every intention of meeting you at the Hermes for a drink. . .

–I'm listening. . .

–Look. I told you. All right, I'm telling you. I was at home, packing for Australia. . .

–Could never have been more than a quick one on your way to Heathrow then, could it?
–Let's leave that aside. I was packing. This phone call from the hospital came out of the blue. Gordon, my mother's had a heart attack. Two. The second was a major one. . .
–You didn't say you were off to the mortuary, so I take it she's pulled through. . .
–Too right she has. They've implanted a pacemaker. . .
Some of Gordon's suspicions are allayed. The hospital story could be checked on and, even to a passer-by, it would be obvious that Harry Plimsoll, stirring his tea endlessly, is a man seriously preoccupied.
–Anything I can do, Harry?
Just for an instant, Harry is touched by this offer. Then he thinks of what he terms the price tag. In days, or less, Gordon could enmesh him with a gentle net from which it would be impossible to extricate himself – unless he vanished to Australia, leaving Gordon to play surrogate son to Margaret.
–Not really, Gordon. Thanks, though. You know, there really is something I'd have told you if we'd managed to make it to the Hermes . . . Gordon, I just don't think we've got enough in common. . .
–Never thought that might be one of the reasons I'm here? To give us some experiences together. . .
–I thought you'd say that . . . It has to be no, Gordon. You're looking for something I just can't offer at present. It's not a question of wanting to . . . it's just circumstances. You're a generous bloke, Gordon. I can't give you the priority you need in someone's life. Look at all these calls on my time. . .
–Can't you explain a bit more, Harry? I'd try and understand. . .
–There you go, see? All this wanting to understand. You're too ready with all the self-sacrificing bit, Gordon, honestly you are. It wouldn't be fair to ask you to start sharing my new burdens. . .
–Is that not what couples are about, Harry? I remember when Blair and I . . . all right, I won't go into that . . . Surely you can tell me about these burdens?
–It's my mother. That just for starters.

Gordon looks at the portrait of dejection that faces him. Harry's hair is in dire need of styling. It's debatable whether he's shaved in the past twenty-four hours. Patches as dark as bruises at the inner corners of the eyes seem to point to a night sleepless with worry. Nervous fingers bend the plastic teaspoon this way and that until it snaps. For Gordon, there's no two ways about it. Harry is a man who needs comfort, however much he may protest.

–Surely your mother's over the worst?
–No . . . that's the problem. For me, this is just the beginning. Look, Gordon, did you manage to catch that film *The Staircase*?
–Can't say that I did. Why? Is it important?
–It is. As a warning. Burton and Rex Harrison played a couple of gay men . . . More or less our age they were supposed to be. From what you've told me, I'd say they were trying to live as the kind of couple you and Blair were. The problem, in the film, I mean, is that the mother of one of them is bedridden and incontinent. She's a sort of millstone round their necks and they're both sinking under the weight . . . Gordon, I wouldn't want that for you, or anyone. You deserve better . . . I must just learn to cope with it alone . . . No. Listen Gordon. I'm not being all noble. It's for me to work out something and try and fit some kind of a life for myself round it. . .
–Surely we could give it a try together, Harry? I wouldn't mind giving a hand with the cooking for us all at the weekends . . . If it's a question of buying one of these washing machines to handle the soiled bed linen, I think I could go halves. . .
–You're a very sweet person, Gordon. I might have guessed you'd say that. You deserve the truth. It's hard, but I won't insult you with anything less . . . Forget me.
–Let's not be dramatic, Harry. Things'll look a lot brighter in a couple of weeks, with the spring coming on. We're neither of us eighty yet. Shouldn't we wait a bit . . . and then talk again?

Harry looks down at his shirt cuff and scratches at a dried globule of egg yolk. The movement eases the fabric back sufficiently to reveal his watch.

–Ever considered going back to Scotland, Gordon?
–Once or twice. There's nothing there for me. And no one, either. . .

–All I'm saying is, don't make me a reason for staying in London. If you really want to find a bit of happiness here, you owe it to yourself to forget me.

No more than a suspicion flits through Gordon's mind. Is Harry giving a superb performance by playing on his sympathies? If he is, then he's a man unscrupulous enough to turn any new event, any trivial circumstance, to his own ends. It is those ends that Gordon still cannot define. What he does register is that Harry is determined to steer the conversation as he wishes.

On impulse, Gordon attempts to regain the initiative.

–That's not as easy as you make it sound, Harry. By the by, the phone number you gave me. It was a disused line. . .

–Well, there you are. Just shows the tension I've been dealing with these past weeks. And now, to cap it all, a dependent mother. Anyway, like I said, there's no point in all that now, Gordon. Heaven knows what time I'll have for any private life. . .

With Harry so set on self-preservation, Gordon accepts he'll make no further headway. All he's left with is the possibility that the enjoyment he's experienced in Harry's company for their two weekends together has been one-sided and self-deluding. To test this he gets up and rebuttons his raincoat.

–Very well then, Harry. If you're determined to shut me out, I'll leave you to it. Maybe I'll try contacting you at work in a week or so. I'm walking this way. . .

Quite astounded for a moment, Harry stares at Gordon. The placid doll, who's danced when his strings have been jerked, has broken free of the cords and, like Coppelia or Pinocchio, asserted some independence. Just as Gordon is about to turn away, Harry manages to smile and shake his head sadly.

–Perhaps, Gordon . . . We'll see . . . Don't hold out any hopes though. . .

Shortly before he reaches Blackfriars Station, Gordon hears laughter for the first time that day. Since a breeze is tossing down raindrops that have collected in the trees above him, he turns only briefly towards the lawns of one of the Inns of Court. Two men by a gardeners' shed are sharing a joke. Gordon wonders whether there isn't something familiar about the younger of the two. The way his nut-brown hair curls over the back of the collar, perhaps? He dismisses this and thinks of Harry again as a sudden gust flings a tiny shower in his face.

☆

Rita Humby inspects each leaf of her begonia rex. The plant, on the window-sill of her living room, has survived more than twenty years without a spot of mould or decay. Had she noticed any, she would have snipped a cutting from the main stem and made a fresh start on this first afternoon of spring. Not that a new plant would ever be the same as the original for Rita. Les bought the begonia. She herself went straight out and found a little sage-green Wedgewood bowl in which to stand it on the very day they'd heard from Noreen that they were to be reunited as a family, and with the baby, too. Somehow, over the years, the begonia has become a sign that Noreen's common sense prevailed and that, despite her rash and tragic marriage, she would be welcome.

As Rita digs around the roots with an old kitchen fork, she hears a jaunty whistle but doesn't bother to look up. With the boys' comprehensive school just beyond her patio wall, she's become used to teenagers attracting the attention of their friends, or any of the girls who might be on their way home from the convent. She welcomes the robust noises of a new generation. They are more welcome than neighbouring pensioners tapping at her door. Only since Len's death has she really begun to understand that requests for a loan of the morning paper, or the use of a screwdriver, are little more than excuses to punctuate the silent hours before evening television begins.

When the whistling becomes more insistent, she supposes a football has bounced down among her tubs of crocus. There'll be another grinning fifteen-year-old straddling the brickwork. Rita prepares to exact her usual bargain. If she returns the ball, then the lad must run to the fish shop on the corner and bring her a bag of chips before he dashes off for the night.

She looks up from her open window to find her grandson doing his Mick Jagger imitation at her patio gate.

–Surprise, surprise. Look what the cat's dragged home. . .

He bops his way across the red and green concrete slabs towards the kitchen door.

–Where you been then, Gran? I've been standing here five minutes. Bet you were fifty years younger, doing the Charleston again. . .

–Better than all this jitter bugging you get up to. Look at that sky. If you don't want to get soaked, go in and put the kettle on. Your legs are younger than mine. Always supposing you can remember where the kettle is. . .

–Now then. No need to get sarkie.

By the time Rita has moved heavily through to the kitchen, Fred has filled the kettle and has perched himself on the draining board. She looks at him, wondering if she's seeing similarities that are really not there. Are there echoes of his grandfather in the way he braces his shoulders, or in the way he lowers his brows as he smiles at her?

–So, Ricky, to what do we owe the honour this time? Bit early for an Easter egg, isn't it?

On the train, approaching Richmond, Fred has prepared himself for the family banter but, as always, refuses to be made guilty by it. His grandmother wouldn't wish it. He knows that. And he knows she wouldn't wish him to think of her as lonely and forgotten. She's happy in her tiny flatlet with its access to a communal dining room and rest lounge whenever she cares to use them.

–Just thought I'd look in. No big deal, is it, coming to see my gran? Did you get the cards I sent? Anyone'd think we didn't have a natter most weeks . . . well, almost every week then. Don't go acting the deserted pensioner. . .

–Fat lot of good that'd do me. Cards and phone calls are all very well, young man. It's what the heck you're getting up to that I wonder about. . .

–Worry about?

–I never said that. You're like the rest of the Humbys, you can look after yourself. What I meant was, who's to say where you are if you're needed? Like the blessed Scarlet Pimpernel you are: *They seek him here, they seek him there*. . .

–I like that. Always thought I was more fanciable than Leslie Howard. . .

–That'll be the day! You'd pass in a crowd, I'll say that for you . . . For how much longer, I wouldn't care to wager. A couple of early nights and a decent meal wouldn't do you any harm, from the looks of you. Where've you come from this time? Walked from John O'Groats?

Not keen to be too precise about his whereabouts, Fred thinks of his recent conversations with Harry – in particular, of the way that his own questions have been parried.

–No, but I keep in training for it. In a manner of speaking, Gran, I've been doing a lot of moving around and not getting very far. Not till very recently. You could put it that way. . .

–That's the price you pay for being a rolling stone. Odd jobs here and hostels there. We never had a gypsy in the family before. . .

–No? What about that six months just after you were married when nobody knew where Grandpa was?

–That was different. . .

–So you say. What was he doing wandering round all those old battlefields in the north of France then?

–You know nothing about that. Just make the tea if you're going to, before the kettle boils its guts out.

Fred does so but he does not intend to be distracted. As he carries a tray through to the living room he speaks over his shoulder.

–I'd be plain bloody stupid not to have worked it out. He was looking for what was left of himself, after losing all his mates at Arras. So, before you say it, I am a bit like him. Been searching for myself, see?

Rita breaks a milk chocolate biscuit and dunks it, bit by bit, in her tea.

–Well, I hadn't thought about it like that. Maybe, Ricky, there's something. . .

Fred puts his cup down very firmly. With both hands on his knees he looks hard at his grandmother.

—How many times have I got to say I won't answer to Ricky any more? I've told you, and I've told mum, I'm Fred. If you call me Ricky you might as well talk to that wall. Sounds like a soft version of . . . you know who. . .
—Your father? Frederick?
—Well, I don't mean Cliffy Richard, do I? Or Frederick the bloody Great?
—Whoever you're talking about, watch your language in this house. If you're keen on being like my Les, just remember your grandfather never swore in front of me in his life.

Remembering many afternoons on his grandfather's allotment when the old man had damned the starlings and the snails to hell, Fred smiles and shrugs, and then pours more tea for them both.

—Did you and Grandpa take it hard when Mum split?
—Split?
—Went to America. . .
—Let's have a drop more milk in this tea and don't ask damn fool questions . . . Fred. Course it was hard. We tried to make the best of it. Les planned a trip out to see you all when he retired. No need to go into what happened all over again. Well, at least we saved the fare and bought the car. The old Bond three-wheeler. Remember it, do you?
—Just about. Remember the first time I went to Brighton in it. We ate Sandwich Spread on the top of the Downs . . . Didn't you like him at all, Gran?
—Your father? . . . Can't say I did. He was your mother's choice and it wasn't for us to interfere. He wasn't the first she'd brought round. There was some lad from the grammar school . . . the name's gone now. Anyway, you're not here to catch up on family history, if I know you. Broke, are you? Want to draw something on those postal orders you keep sending me from here, there and everywhere?
—Wrong, see? I'm here for a celebration. Got you a large bar of Cadbury's milk with nuts and raisins. Here . . . Go on, take your teeth out, if you want. I know the nuts get under your plate.
—You cheeky monkey. You've got your grandfather's humour, I'll say that. . .

The tone is affectionate. Rita knows her grandson will warm to any comparison with Les. More than one neighbour, she recalls, had mentioned after the funeral they'd seldom seen a teenager so broken with grief. Something no one would have expected in a boy.

–Not going to ask me what we're celebrating, Gran?

–Let's think . . . Got yourself a girl at last but not a penny to bless yourselves with?

Fred answers without a pause. It's a question he's half-expected. The ritual answer has served him well enough in lodgings and bars and he doesn't think it will be rejected with a probing glance.

–Time for all that later. No, this is far better news.

–Won the pools? More than my Les ever did in twenty-five years. . .

–Gave him something to do on winter evenings, didn't it?

–Stop pinching my words, young Fred, or I'll clump your ears, big as you are . . . I give up. Tell us what we're celebrating, then you can go and fetch us some chips. They won't be serving left-overs from lunch by now. . .

–Good thinking. We'll have chips. And I'm doing the paying. Fact is, I've got a job . . . in London. . .

–Have you now? Told your mother yet?

–She'll get a card in due course . . . Want to know what I'll be doing?

–Nothing that'll get you into a collar and tie, I'll be bound.

–Too right. It's gardening. . .

–Gardening? What the heck do you know about roses and chrysanths?

–Come on, Gran. Who coped with Grandpa's allotment when his asthma got too bad? Anyway, how d'you know what I've been up to lately? I could have been on evening courses. . .

–I'd rather not think what half of you get up to these days. All these programmes about pop stars with drugs . . . these discos, or whatever they're called, where there's men dancing with men . . . whatever next?

Fred watches his grandmother's face as she speaks. There's no condemnation despite the words. He attributes this to the bewilderment of the old when faced with any new phenomena. Just for a moment he wonders if he too, in a new century, might be equally confused by fresh ideas and developments in technology.

–You can forget all that so far as I'm concerned. I've never been penniless on the streets. Never will be.

–Be that as it may. So, it's gardening, eh? Who's been daft enough to let you loose on the parks then? I'd best use my bus pass to take a squint before you ruin it with something you've mugged up in a library. . .

Instantly wary, Fred lights a cigarette and smiles before he replies. There's no way he's going to help his relatives trace his whereabouts until he chooses to let them know.

–So, who said anything about parks? Might be Buckingham Palace. There again, could be one of the museums.

–Just so long as it isn't down the riverside among all those roughs. Lousy with bugs they are, if you're to believe what you see on television. Setting fire to themselves as well, with bottles of meths. What do they think they are, Buddhist monks?

Fred laughs and helps himself to a chunk of the present he's brought. Rita slaps his wrist good-humouredly.

–No need to lose sleep over me, Gran. I've always looked after myself. . .

–So, whose choice was that? You could have stayed with me when Les died. I'd have made a home for us all in Cranesview Terrace. Your mother could have come down when she'd got days off. . .

–That's all ifs now, Gran. Here. I'll buzz along and get us those chips. . .

–Yes, I suppose it is all ifs . . . If you like, Fred, you could have a shake-down on the couch. That is, if you're minded to stay over . . . Suppose you'll want to be off with your mates, to celebrate. . .

Jubilant that he's fixed a job not ten minutes' walk from where Harry lives, and rather less from Fleet Street, Fred feels inclined to mention to his grandmother that he intends to buy a couple of bottles of beer and call on his new friend. Nothing more specific than a reference to a journalist he's met.

He's about to do so when a disturbing thought deters him. First, he has no phone number and might have to sit some time on the doorstep. Second – and this unsettles him more – might Harry

arrive home with someone else? A rival who'd been out of town while Harry was dallying near the coffee stall?
It's something he needs to think through by himself.
–Since when did I start going in for crowds, Gran? I had sort of promised a journalist mate of mine I'd drop by. . .
–Journalists, is it now? . . . Well, watch him, whoever he is. Don't believe half he says, even when he's sober. And, another thing, watch he pays his way. All out to get something for nothing, that lot . . . Saw enough of journalists when I used to help out with the catering at rugby matches.
–Don't cosset me, Gran. I've been around. I've got my eyes open . . . Here, what you fiddling with your purse for? . . . I'm paying, remember? Don't pretend your mind's going . . . Bright as a new pin you are. . .
–What's all the flattery? When you get to my age, young Fred, you're lucky to know if it's Christmas or Tuesday, some mornings . . . Go on then. You buy the chips and I'll stand us a nice bit of cod. Watch he doesn't palm you off with something that's all batter, too. Can't trust these Cypriots like the old London fish-fryers. . .
–Watch it, Gran! Watch it! Whose own grannie came from Milan if I'm not mistaken? Give me ten minutes and you can start carving the bread and butter. I could murder half a loaf by myself. . .
Under the patio light, Fred, counting his change to be sure he's sufficient for a phone call if directory enquiry can find the number, drops a coin. In retrieving it, his glance is distracted by a terra cotta flower trough. The earth is sodden and only the lifeless stalks of a few dahlias remain. Empty, he's sure he could carry the trough in both arms as far as the station. It would – and he visualises the finished effect – make an eye-catching feature if filled with geraniums and lobelia. Quite a treat to look out on, through a kitchen window, whether the sun happened to be shining or more rain continued to saturate the gardens.

☆

Harry's first impression is that he's walking into another of the small film studios around Soho in which he's done voice-overs from time to time. His second follows on. He wouldn't be surprised to find a technical crew moving out with sufficient film in the can to launch a campaign for *Be Kind To Grandma Week*. His mother, supported among a snowy range of pillows, sits upright in her bed facing the door. He more than suspects that an easy chair facing the picture window has recently been occupied. This would explain why he's been kept waiting at the seventh floor landing. The patient has been settled so that she shall look her best. In Harry's mind there's no doubt that Margaret herself has added a telling detail here and there.

There's no evidence of hospital clothing. Margaret's favourite night-dress has been freshly laundered and ironed. Since the sky is already darkening above Westminster, a bedside light has been turned on. This emphasises the soft folds of the pink flannelette. Harry's eye lingers on a double band of daisies embroidered across the bust. Daisies again. He recalls them being in vases everywhere when he was a child, remembers them as pattern round the borders of a tablecloth, and he has an image of Margaret wrapping gifts in paper specially ordered at the stationers. Daisies seem to have formed a leitmotif for his mother.

Margaret stares at him in silence. She then lifts her right hand with a frail hesitancy that would be the envy of any actress playing a distressed archduchess. Though he tries to resist it, Harry's attention is drawn to Margaret's hair, just as she intends. The change wrought by the hospital hairdresser's determination can only be called a triumph. The mop of tangled rope that Harry had glimpsed from the doorway has been replaced by an aureole of lilac-tinted curls.

Returning her stare, Harry thinks she lacks nothing but a linen cap and horn-rimmed glasses. He could then be cast as Little Red Riding Hood come visiting. Except that he bears no gifts.

He turns away to close the door before approaching the foot of the bed. As he does so he murmurs quite audibly.

–Bloody old she-wolf.

There's no reaction.

Fortified by cards from well-wishers and flanked by a battalion of flowers, Margaret regards her visitor with all the assurance of a general commanding the high ground. Her teeth, steeped for days in cleansing solution, are now back in her head. She bares them at Harry in a smile as benign as that she'd offered earlier to Amanda, who'd begun with such amusing questions that had developed, for Margaret, into a tiresome probing.

Harry's fascination is torn between the dentures that underline his fanciful image of a she-wolf in grannie drag, and the gash of lipstick his mother has very obviously insisted on applying for herself. No nurse, he's sure, could have sketched a Cupid's bow so garish as to suggest a temptress who'd strayed from the cutting-room floor of the silent film era.

The silence continues. Both participants know the rules of the power war and have become, over the years, well acquainted with most of each other's strategies. Margaret opens the contest by summoning up her limpid look. Her dark eyes have not faded with age but they have, in recent years, become more adept in conveying a mood of long suffering and great goodness. It's not inferior to that assumed by Lady Diana Cooper in old photographs of a production of *The Miracle*.

Since he knows it well, Harry remains unmoved by this, Margaret, confident of her advantageous position, makes the initial foray. She presses her fingertips together on the coverlet so that the lacquer sparkles in the subdued lighting. And then she speaks in a tiny voice.

–Your mother would like just a sip of that orange juice . . .
–She would?

Margaret's sigh is hardly audible.

–If her son had a grain of humanity in him, he'd pour it for her. She hasn't the strength to reach out to that table at the moment. . . One day . . . maybe . . .

–If my mother has the strength to daub her face with lipstick and pat her hair, she can damn well pour her own orange juice. . . Here . . .

A couple of strides bring him to the wheeled table. In a trice, he's rammed it against the bedside and resumed his confrontational position.

–You unnatural boy . . . always were. I'll do without . . .

–Up to you. I've no doubt there'll be some young nurse popping in any moment ready to do your bidding . . .
–Must I rely on strangers in my old age?
–They're paid for it. If it didn't give them a warm glow, they wouldn't do it . . .
–You hard-boiled creature. I could lie here and rot as far as you're concerned, Little Beast.

Harry responds with a shrug, and begins to beat his fingers in an unrhythmic tattoo on the ironwork of the bed rail. A solution to the immediate problem appears to strike him. He offers it to Margaret in a let's discuss-this-amicably tone.

–Tell you what. Why don't you come clean with this hospital gang. . . Tell them your son rejects you? That's the jargon. If you tell them that, they'll have to log it. Probably underline it three times in red. Outrage them a bit, and we'll get some action . . . They'd find you a perch in the best geriatric home in town when you get out of here . . .
–You unfeeling swine. . . When I get out? . . . If I ever do . . .
–When, old She-Wolf. When. They know it. I know it, and so do you.

It's a shrewd lunge on Harry's part and one that silences Margaret for a moment. It has always been she who's used the geriatric home as an emotional ace of trumps. In the silence, she produces a lace handkerchief, but uses it – unpredictably – to dab her fingertips, not her eyes.

–Think you can frighten me, Little Beast? . . . And don't think I haven't noticed you won't sit down. . . Not comfortable here, eh? . . . Pity I didn't die, isn't it? . . . But then, it might have been for the best . . . I wouldn't have been a burden to you all . . . Interrupting your plans for Europe. Was Europe, wasn't it? . . . Can't think why the nurses were on about Australia . . .
–Crap. A burden to us all? Crap. You haven't a spoonful of empathy in your body. And don't think that prayer book among the roses'll fool me. I'm not one of your Irish nurses . . .
–You'll remember that when you see me dead in my coffin. Not one thought for the mother who gave you life . . .
–Oh, come on. Spare us the Mother McCree string quartet. Tell you something. Took me years to work out how you could bring yourself to suffer the indignities of a maternity home.

You didn't want me. . . Couldn't bear others to think you were barren, that's what that was all about . . .
—You monster. Worse than Caligula, you are. You should have had my brothers for a father. They'd have taken a strap to you . . .
Harry yawns – quite openly – from boredom. He knows this part of Margaret's repertoire only too well.
—I don't doubt it. As I've always said, you come from an outstanding family of Calvinists. What they lacked in affection they made up for in a bit of licensed sado-masochism . . .
—Get out. Go on, leave me. I'm tired of your smart talk. You're sicker than I am. Go and try your nonsense on the doctors, and you'll wonder what's hit you. Words aren't going to solve your problem in the coming weeks, Little Beast.
Seeming to dismiss him, Margaret rests her eyes and folds her hands on her chest. She can't quite decide whether it had been Flora Robson or Anna Neagle who'd once played such an effective death in a British historical film.
Harry watches, smiling. He studies her eyelids and ignores the rest. Noting that they're not quite closed, he gets ready to sharpen his tone.
—The coming weeks don't worry me one little bit. It's the years. Your dream of having me as an unpaid servant till I'm fifty. That is something I won't bloody well tolerate. . . Get this into your scheming head, old She-Wolf. . . I've got one life . . .
—Without me you'd have had none . . .
—As I was saying, I've got one life – for which I didn't ask – and if you have to go to the wall so I can get on with it, then that is how it's going to be . . .
—If your poor father could hear you now . . .
—Don't drag him on to play a bit-part. You just lie there and remember how you worked him into the ground. Oh, yes. Every weekend doing your house repairs, keeping that damn great garden as a showpiece for your friends. . . Even fetching your shopping when you wanted to do your Grand Duchess number with your feet up, guzzling chocolate creams and paperback romances in equal proportions . . .
The dark eyes snap open in what Margaret hopes will be as terrifying a way as Edith Evans' did in *The Queen of Spades*.

This is not as effective as it should be, for Harry has also seen the film.

–You monstrosity. You're a perversion from your tinted hair to those green suede boots, that's what you are. My own mother knew it when she first looked at you. Know what she called you?

–Nothing pleasant, that's for sure . . .

–That's it. Go on. Insult the dead. They can't answer you, and I don't suppose I shall for much . . .

–Don't excite yourself, or you won't enjoy your supper. What did she call me?

–A changeling. That's what she said, and she wasn't wrong.

There's a look in Margaret's eye that troubles Harry. Always keen to be in possession of as many facts as he can before engaging in argument, he feels Margaret has some reserve troops of whose existence he's been ignorant. Best, he feels, to show no interest, wait and see what's revealed. Meanwhile, he shifts his ground.

–Your mother, wrong? She never was, according to you. Probably telling her God He's enjoying himself too much at this moment. Meanwhile, old She-Wolf, let's tackle the problem. Me and you. We're as tough as each other . . . and as perceptive. Unlike you, however, I'm not a manipulative person . . .

Margaret's laugh is derisive. She's as expert at it as a coloratura sailing through a cadenza. Not every coloratura has had three quarters of a century in which to perfect her craft.

–You? . . . Not manipulative? . . . You make me laugh. Go on, get out of my sight and find yourself one of those odd creatures you hang around with. At least Benjamin Britten and his fancy man don't go looking for flotsam and jetsam half the night. Don't think I haven't worked it out for myself. . . Go on, you tire me . . . I'll look after myself. That nice woman who works here at night will make enquiries for me. There's an address in *The Daily Telegraph* for distressed gentlefolk. . . Not that you'll ever need it. Get out, Little Beast . . .

And Harry does move, but not to the door. He sits on the window-sill, not displeased that he flattens two or three cards from well-wishers in doing so. By the lights above the hospital's main entrance, he traces a pattern in the early tulips that are in

flower on either side of the concrete approach. The gardener, he surmises, must have been trained in the armed forces. What other imagination would have used tulips to reproduce the hospital's flag as floral decorations?
–Do as you think fit about that, old She-Wolf. . . Ever tried to work out why it is I can offer kindness to men you know nothing about? Apart from Gordon, you've scarcely even met them . . .
–Kindness? It's more than any of us have ever seen.
–Correction. More than you've seen much of. Tell you why. Because it's something you've never offered me.
–Twaddle. How dare you speak of kindness – prepared to treat your own mother in this inhuman way?
–For a bloody good reason. I've seen how you operate. Given an opening smaller than a gnat's nostril, you're in there and using anyone. Don't bother closing your eyes again. I'll have my say and then I'm off. You've used everyone who's drifted into your orbit. Particularly Father.
The eyes open once more. They flash, this time, with real anger. Like some crone in a forgotten melodrama, Margaret waves her index finger and, as she speaks, spittle drips over her lipstick.
–That's a lie and you know it. I worked these fingers raw to give you and your father a decent home.
–What a curtain line! You worked to be admired. All you wanted to hear, from anyone who dropped in, was praise for what Margaret had made, or sewn or cooked. That's what that was about. Finish.
–And, of course, I gave you nothing?
–Nothing I needed. I didn't want birthday spreads for others to admire. Don't you bloody understand?. . . Look, some women neglect their kids for their husbands. With others it's the reverse. But you, old She-Wolf, you had to be something different. You neglected us both to love yourself. All we ever were to you were servants in a fantasy.
This rekindles the flame in Margaret's eyes and voice. She is no longer a heap of ashes and yesterdays. Fury reddens the ruched skin of her neck.
–Explain yourself!. . . Servants?
–Seem to have scored a hit, eh? I mean, you old predator, that when you left Mombassa fifty years ago, there were twelve

flunkies waving you off. You've been looking for them ever since. Make the nurse who brings your supper one. Turn your home help into another. . . Me? I'm not for hire.
—You should be horsewhipped.
—I should have thought that'd be too good for me. You've missed a cliché . . .
Genuinely tired by her brief outburst, Margaret changes to a less demanding role. She sniffs nobly, shaking her curls to indicate that she'll not give way to tears. It's not a bad echo of Sybil Thorndike's performance in *Waiting In the Wings* which, with sherry-sodden Winnie, she'd seen at a matinée just before Christmas 1960.
As an afterthought, she touches the outer corners of her eyes with her little finger. Dame Sybil couldn't have bettered that.
—The word Mother means nothing to you. I see that. Well, Little Beast, the years soon roll round. You'll be eighty, and alone, one day . . . if some of these social diseases don't get you first . . .
—Are we standing by for the witch's curse?
—I leave you to your conscience. Think of what you've said to me, if you bother to come to my funeral. . .
—I'm worried about you coming to mine.
—I'd not care to rub shoulders with those who do.
Harry checks his watch. With luck, Noreen will have the sherry bottle out in a few minutes. More pressing, he realises, is a need to eat something. It irks him that, for a second time, he's trapped in the hospital at close on dinner time.
He gets up, stretches, yawns ostentatiously and walks towards the door. Half-way there he pauses.
—By the way, who's Alastair?
The first reaction is a glare so intense that it conjures up for him some childhood misdemeanour. This time he does not lower his gaze.
—Well, old She-Wolf, who is he? One of the staff here said he was some sort of a cousin. News to me. . .
—Some sort of a cousin or not, he'd have shown more compassion than my own son. . .
—That's pushing it a bit, isn't it? You can have the compassion I'd show anyone of your age. No more; no less. Family, to me, is just an accident. . . Who's Alastair?

–Get out before I have to crawl across this floor and ring for help...
–You'd do it better than Vivien Leigh in *Gone With The Wind*, I'm sure... Who's Alastair?
–Someone whose name you're not fit to mention. Out.
–I'll drop by when I've got a spare hour. I expect to see you standing on your own two feet again. You'll not get the chance to stand on mine.
–Out! You monster...
–Have the last word if it'll shut you up.

☆

For more than twenty minutes Fred has been concentrating on geraniums. By the light of the street lamp he flicks through a series of colour shots illustrating single and double varieties. He concentrates on suggestions for massing them in eye-catching beds: flame-tinted blooms edged with cream, contrasted with deeper-toned specimens rich as boiled beetroot. As he thumbs the pages repeatedly, hints once grunted to him by his grandfather recur. Very soon, Fred's confident he could become an expert on geraniums, much sought after by local authorities in the London area. Membership of the relevant Society – he's sure there must be one – becomes a priority just as soon as he can afford the subscription.

Aware that a passer-by has paused to stare down at him he pretends total absorption in the well-worn book he bought at a market stall in Lower Marsh, on his way to his grandmother's. Flicking a page, Fred allows his eyes to study the pair of shoes not a footstep from his own. They're barely flecked by mud or rain.

Fred's glance edges up. The well-pressed grey flannels appear to have been chosen for their anonymity in a crowd. He wonders if it might be the chucker-out, Harry's neighbour, and prepares an explanation for his own presence in the sheltered doorway. It buoys his confidence that, despite the weather, he's unlikely to be mistaken for a down-and-out seeking admission

at the Rowton House hostel by the Elephant and Castle. If the grey flannels allow their wearer to pass unnoticed among the white-collared workers then – so Fred reasons – his own blue jeans should seem no more than the uniform of London's younger generations.
–Waiting for someone, young man?
The tone of voice is recognisable instantly to Fred. He doesn't need to look up to know he'll confront a detective; one probably based at the police station around the corner. He replies jauntily, careful to repress the truculence he feels.
–What's that to you, mate?
He expects an identity card to be produced and uses his momentary advantage to decide that he'll do his best to avoid implicating Harry, should whatever follows turn sour.
–Satisfied, lad? What're you doing here, eh?
–Matter of fact, Officer, I'm expecting a mate of mine any minute.
–Expecting you, is he?
–Course. . . He's a journalist. . .
Fred hopes the allusion to a profession, rather than a trade – and a profession not easily inhibited – might keep the conversation on a manageable level.
–His wife not at home to let you in?
Not the flicker of an eye from Fred; no hesitation, either.
–No one in yet.
The detective lights a cigarette and changes tack.
–Not from this manor, are you?
–Yes and no, in a manner of speaking, Officer. Been staying in a hostel over the water. Getting a place of my own now. . .
–Working then?
Fred closes his paperback so that the cover will show in the lamplight. The line of questioning isn't foreign to him and he's pleased that he's able to anticipate each move in the ritual. The middle-class trick of addressing any policeman as an officer seems to be working.
–Working? . . . Just started over in those gardens by the Law Courts. . . Doing my homework like a good boy. Standard work on bedding plants, this is. . .
–What's your name, then?

–Ricky. Ricky Humby. . .
–Right then, Ricky Humby. I'll be passing again in about an hour. Dare say your mate will have let you in by then. Not the weather for sitting about studying flowers, is it? . . . This mate of yours, would he be a gardening correspondent?
–No. He does all sorts. . .
–So, what've you got in common then?
–Enough. Soccer . . . he's a Millwall fanatic. Me, I'm Brentford. . .
Fred's sigh of relief as the detective laughs has to be silent. With luck, they're heading away from troubled waters.
–Millwall? . . . Brentford? . . . A right couple of no-hopers, the pair of you, from the sound ot it. I'll leave you to console each other. . .
–Night, Officer.
Watching until the detective is out of earshot, Fred farts with all the power that he can extract from a pickle sandwich and two lagers consumed at the Waterloo Bar. For good measure he waves two fingers of either hand at the back of the retreating figure.
Only as he starts to fumble for his tobacco pouch does Fred notice his fingers are trembling and that sweat is trickling from his armpits. It's a small price to pay for coping with the police again; this time successfully.
So he grins as he licks a cigarette paper and reviews the recent conversation. The invention of an interest in soccer he judges to have been a master-stroke. *Tell 'em what they want to hear*. The advice, given to him years earlier by a convicted street-trader, was no scrap of idle chatter on the steps of a magistrates' court. Fred's grin turns to a chuckle as he considers the probable effect on the detective had he been told that ballet, hair-styling and oral sex were the topics most touched on in conversations with Harry.
Big Ben striking nine is just about audible through the rain. Counting steadily, Fred accepts that Harry must be eating out and isn't likely to be home for an hour or so. It does cross his mind that he knows very little about the man. Who does? Could the house be under surveillance, he wonders, and the detective have been playing a subtler game? Fred thinks this unlikely,

though he does recall Harry, during breakfast, mentioning that such men as themselves have always been an easy conviction whenever statistics need boosting at police stations. Although he laughed this off as history, Fred remembers Harry cutting him short by adding something about the viciousness with which some policemen reacted, once the law was changed, and they were deprived of easy prey. He wonders if some of Harry's bitterness might be rooted in a past arrest or even imprisonment.

And then he chuckles again, with two passing vagrants as audience. Technically, he and Harry have already blown a raspberry at the amended law. Only Harry's closed bedroom door separated them from the bouncer and the retired policeman. It was not locked, in a land where no lock meant no sex, let alone affection. With every intention of flouting such a law again in a matter of hours, Fred decides to find out just a little more about Harry's neighbours. Since one of them is a retired policeman, it's a question of calculating the risk, rather than nosiness, that prompts him to jump up and press the lower bell.

More than three minutes elapse before a light is switched on somewhere to the rear of the passageway. The sound of carpet slippers shuffling over linoleum becomes audible. The door unbolted, it's opened wide enough for Fred to look down on a chalk-white face crowned by a few damp wisps of hair. In the dimness, a security chain glitters at chest level. It adorns the old man's dressing-gown like a ceremonial necklace.

–What you selling?

–Selling? Nothing . . . Look, sorry to disturb you at an awkward moment. . .

–Tell us what you want . . . I was just getting out of the bath. Friday night's bath night. I keep to the routine, even though Mrs Duke's been gone five years. . .

Already surprised that the old man has to peer up rather that meet him eye-to-eye, Fred's more than puzzled by what he's just been told. The wizened pensioner could never have been tall enough to have been a policeman. And just who is, or was, Mrs Duke?

Fred risks an outside chance.

–Sorry to hear about your wife.

–Mustn't complain. We had forty years together. A fine woman, was Mrs Duke . . . Don't know how much longer I'll be able to carry on by myself round here. Not so comfortable as it used to be for the likes of us, see? The street's being gentrified. That's what they call it on the television programmes. Gentrified . . . There's a headmaster in that place opposite. Wouldn't credit it, would you? . . . There again, there's Mr Plimsoll got the upstairs here. It's all change, isn't it . . . Anyway, you collecting for something?

–Collecting? . . . Only for myself. Fact is, I'm keeping an eye open for a room round here. Just started a new job, ten minutes' walk away. Know of anything going?

–Can't help you, mate . . . You'd do better asking him upstairs. He's the landlord, after all. He might know. One of the new ones he is. Journalist. Got a woman comes in and cleans for him. I hear him at it . . . only if I happen to be passing the bottom of the stairs, you understand? *Would you mind doing the study and the dining room today, Lil?* That's him. Not like the old days when Mrs Duke and I were glad of a couple of rooms over the jellied eel shop in the market . . . If it was like that, still, I mean, you might be lucky, mate. Can't be sure of anything these days . . . Try him upstairs, as I say, he might be considering someone permanent. Make a change from all these comings and goings . . . Use the other bell next time. I don't answer to a living soul once the news is over.

–Right. I'll do that. Mr Plimsoll, was it? . . . Thanks anyway. . .

–Good luck, mate. . .

Fred doesn't wait for the door to close before turning away into the rain. He exults in it. He spurns the poor shelter of newly budding trees along the main road. He ignores what protection there is from shop doorways, and from hoardings where terraced cottages are being razed to make way for tower blocks. He bounds through pools, not over them. He's not yet twenty-four and he's found a man with whom he wants to share some living and some laughter.

It's not going to be easy, Fred knows. Then he adds to himself, as he shakes his wet hair at a passing bus, it's the challenge Harry's wariness presents that will be the fun of it. If Harry

Plimsoll wants to invent neighbours, so be it. Fred's as ready to play games.

He leapfrogs over traffic bollards and exults in water that splashes up over his legs and down again onto the ragwort and couch grass beginning to appear between cracked pavements. As he does so, he lists his own assets. There's independence, a determination not to plan his days around Harry. That, he's sure, will calm some fears. There's a healthy complexion and a presentable enough body. They'll do for a start, and for a few more years, if he watches the beers, the pies, and the sugar. Most of all, he thinks, as he begins to climb the long slope towards Waterloo Station, there's an eagerness to persuade Harry – in a slow and casual way – that there are happenings to be enjoyed, fresh places to be experienced. Put another way, Fred thinks, Harry needs to be coaxed from settling into middle age.

The left luggage office is about to close for the night.

Fred vaults onto the counter, mimes holding up the steel shutter that's being wound down over his head, and shouts to the duty clerk.

–Call me Samson, mate. I've come for the window-box over there.

–Samson all right. You could do with a bloody haircut like the rest of your bunch. Know what'd cure the lot of you? A good spell in the army, same as I had. This the one?

–Course it is. Didn't think you were running a new line in garden accessories.

–Less of your lip. Here you are then. Now piss off. . .

–Excuse me. You wouldn't have such a thing as a bit of paper, would you?

–They've got paper in the toilets if you're desperate.

–No, listen. I've got to write a note to go with this, see? Present for an old lady who won't see another Easter. Her cat's just been put down, and her only son's being held on suspicion for singing *Cockles and Mussels* at a demo. . .

–You break my bleedin' heart, you do. These leaflets're all we've got. Blank on one side, if that's any good. . .

–Queen, King and Ace . . . Wouldn't happen to have an envelope, too?

–This isn't bloody Woolworths. Just piss off, will you? I got a train to catch.

☆

Noreen chatters excitedly as she produces a bottle and tumblers from a wall cabinet labelled Emergencies Only. Her almost skittish mood, Harry surmises, is to be accounted for by an imminent departure for Greece, not his own arrival. He notes a suitcase, battered but neatly tagged, in a corner by the office door.
–What kept you, Harry? I've been waiting for this for hours . . . They told me you left your mother's room about eight . . . Not been snooping to do a story on the hospital, I hope?
–Told you, I'm not into medical stories . . . No . . . Had to eat something, that's all. Not much choice round Waterloo, is there?
–Should have thought you'd have had time to pop home and knock up something . . . Here.
Harry takes the sherry and they toast each other with a smile.
–To your holiday, Noreen . . . Don't do much cooking for myself . . . unless I've got someone staying. . .
–Bit like me, really. That goes for the sherry as well. Any excuse to open the bottle, that's me. Let's hope I'm not taking after that aunt of yours . . . Minnie, is it?
–Winnie. Shouldn't think you're likely to follow Winnie into Wonderland. Calls herself Lady Plimsoll now. . .
–You're joking?
–No. She has long conversations with the Queen and the Pope. Incontinence of the imagination. Probably terminal.
Judging Harry's banter to be a indication of a more relaxed mood, Noreen decides to probe a little. It might be her only opportunity. By the time she herself is back from holiday, ties with the Plimsoll family are likely to be flimsy.
–I've thought a bit about you, Harry, these past few days.
Harry can think of no reason to be wary. At most, he doesn't expect to see Noreen Humby again more than twice a year for a drink, or a bit of spaghetti.

—And?
—And how life might be for you at forty-plus . . . Not being the marrying kind, as they say. . .
Maybe Harry's laugh is a little over-hearty, especially since he raises his shoulders and lifts his elbows in parody of a Gallic gesture. Noreen waves aside the cigarette he offers and waits.
—All right, Noreen. If I don't tell you now that I'm gay, when do I tell you? . . . You know what I mean?
—I didn't when we were teenagers. Of course I do now . . . Not that I see you leading any of these demonstrations we read about. No, shouldn't think you're into banners. . .
—Too bloody true. You get more done in England over dinner, or a drink.
—That's as may be . . . You should know. Anyway, what about you? Been living like a monk all these years?
—There've been a few. Apart from casuals . . . I dunno, Noreen. Maybe I've always looked for too much in common . . . and then got fed up with staring at a mirror. . .
—Mmm . . . Sue and I always thought you fancied Paul Harding . . . Now he's in Australia . . . you planned to go there . . . Am I right off-beam?
Listening to her, Harry relives, at break-neck speed, a couple of afternoons at the end of the war. His own teenage body, and Paul Harding's, edging closer after swimming somewhere out in Berkshire . . . then the sudden wrenching apart; the awkward suggestion that they should cycle off for a beer.
—Way off, Noreen. It would have been an experiment for Paul while Sue happened to be away. . .
—And for you?
—Didn't arise. There was someone none of you knew about. . .
—Harry Plimsoll! You were two-timing me! Innocent little Noreen thinking your sex life was one long assault course to get your hands on my tits!
—You had nice tits . . . And you had the mountie. . .
—Set and match to you, Harry. . .
They both laugh at a mutual deception practised so long ago. Noreen wonders if some friendship could be developed now between them. It would need to be based on more than a ritual exchange of memories.

–So, the mountie with the bounty? Do tell. . .
–In a sec. One last question, Harry. It's just that we seem to be doing fine. We might meet again. I might even turn up for a drink with some other bloke. Wouldn't want to play triangles by bringing someone you fancied. . .
–Make sure they're tall, willowy, and with shirts made for them in Jermyn Street. I might take the piss out of them, but they're all yours. . .
–I'll remember . . . Ever take anyone home to meet Margaret?
–Tried it once or twice. They started talking recipes. I can do without alliances like that. . .
–She's a handful, isn't she? Get on with your life, Harry. She'll survive. . .
–Thanks for saying that . . . But I haven't forgotten the mountie.

There's a longer silence than any since Harry arrived. After a moment or so, he pushes his cigarette pack across the coffee table. Hesitating only briefly, Noreen takes one.

–Wish I could. Forget the mess he left me in, I mean. . .
–All was not well in the log cabin among the pines?
–Never even saw one! He got me as far as the States as a post-war bride, and there we stayed. We were traipsing round California when I found I was pregnant with Ricky. . .
–Noreen, you're not breaking it to me gently that the mountie was gay? Bisexual, maybe. . .
–Anything but . . . I was getting the sausages ready for tea one afternoon when a dowdy little woman rang the bell . . . Have you guessed yet? . . . The bastard had been married before he ever sailed for Europe. I was the bigamous Mrs Mountie and Ricky was born the wrong side of the blanket, as my mother would say. To be fair, she never did. . .
–What a shit . . . What did you do?
–Came back just as soon as we could get a berth. At least Mr Bloody Woodward paid my fare. And a few hundred besides, on condition I didn't take him to court. I kept the name while Ricky was going through school, for his sake. Now I'm Humby again.
–What's become of him?
–Woodward? How the hell should I know or care?
–No. Forget him . . . Ricky, your son. . .
–He's around. Hit a sticky patch just after Father died. Ricky

idolised his grandfather. He's doing well enough. I don't mean money-wise . . . Who cares about all that, he says, with inflation and nuclear threats . . . Well, that's his way of looking at things. Never in one place more than a month at a time, mind . . . But he remembers my birthday . . . And my mother tells me fresh flowers just appear on Father's grave every now and again. . .
—Didn't realise your father. . .
—It's five years now. Asthma and bronchitis. There was always a weakness after he was gassed on the Western Front . . . Anyway, Ricky was off with a rucksack less than six months after the funeral. . .
—Independent little bugger, eh?
—What would you expect? I get cards from all over the place. But he keeps his nose clean. One brush with the law was enough. A bit of petty pilfering it was. Our psychiatrist here got us through . . . Bet you didn't know shoplifting can be a scream for attention, did you?
—Anne Bancroft in *The Pumpkin Eater*?
—Right! Never thought of that. . .
—So, where's Ricky now? Still wandering?
—Who's to say? . . . It's his life. He's not a child.
—Noreen, I caught you looking at your watch. Time I was pushing off. . .
—Journalists can come to wrong conclusions, Harry. If you want to know, I was thinking this is a record. It is, you know. Not a single interruption from this wretched bleeper. . .
—You win. But I should be making a move, anyway . . . Tell me, now you've finished that second glass, would you risk marrying Dimitri?
—Once was enough, thanks very much. The arrangement with Dimitri suits us both fine . . . It's something I've never talked to Ricky about, and I'd like to now. Maybe I will . . . whenever I do see him. . .
—You've never thought of . . . well, after Dimitri?
—Always told myself I'd not bother again. Perhaps it's the sherry talking but, if anything did go wrong, I just might risk another . . . what shall I say? . . . loose arrangement? I just enjoy the anticipation of someone being around. Sounds a bit like a

thought for the day, Harry. You could try it, and let me know how you get on!

Accepting that this is the pay-off, and that any closer contact will entail another meeting, Harry gathers his cigarettes and throws his raincoat over his shoulder.

–Been thinking of it for years, Noreen. It's doing it that scares the shit out of me. Well, that, and all the pain of the undoing if it goes wrong . . . again.

–So it's premature retirement at forty-plus . . . Come on, Harry. Go and get on with it. When you've found him . . . perhaps when he's found you, bring him to supper. Don't get your knickers in a twist. I'm not out to convert wayward gays. Christ, what a phrase! One more sherry and I'd never manage it.

–Enjoy Greece. I mean the out of bed bit, too . . . Incidentally, did you get anything more on the mysterious Alastair?

–Not a lot. Someone who chatted to your mother said Margaret went all uptight and awkward when his name was mentioned. He's probably been kicking up the daisies for years . . . dead and gone with the long colonial summer.

–Not for her.

Noreen, half-smiling, frowns at Harry's troubled look. Impulsively, and to his amazement, she kisses him on either cheek as she propels him to the door. He pauses to speak but the desk phone rings, and they have to content themselves with an easy wave.

☆

Sprays of flowering prunus look bloodless in the light of a hazy moon. Not that Gordon, flat on his back, notices them at all. He is, when he opens his eyes, aware of the moon appearing and disappearing between scudding clouds. Every fifteen minutes or so he flicks a half-smoked cigarette into the shadows. Sometimes he follows its course and registers that there are bushes almost obscuring a ragstone wall. After thirty minutes, or thereabouts, he notices a cluster of yellow buds hanging not too far from his head, and becomes fancifully jealous of a landscape that's responding without agony or joy to the changing season.

Using his elbow as a lever, he heaves himself up to rest his neck against the stone behind him. Once settled, he checks the level in his whisky bottle, and reconsiders what possible demands there might be for his skills in either Holland or Scandinavia. To be a carpenter with no language other than English is better, he's always maintained, than to be a linguist without a craft. Leaving England is possibility he's often discussed, but the discussions were with Blair.

The urge to start afresh in a different setting has to be weighed now, for Gordon, against a feeling of guilt that he would be abandoning Blair Brodie. Whether Blair might have wished it is something Gordon can never know since death seemed so remote to them both.

Very sure that he's going to continue this circular debate with himself for a long time yet, Gordon fumbles for his whisky bottle and then taps it, with the regularity of a bell, against the headstone behind him.

–Little to report tonight, old darling . . . Spotted a cyclist wearing shorts along by the river. No doubt he got soaked before he was half-way home. The legs were not s'bad at all. Never saw the face. Always cared for a well-turned leg . . . Ate spaghetti in that place by the old tower . . . one we always meant to try . . . I need advice, Blair. Tell you what's troubling me . . . How would it be if our positions were reversed? Would y'be lying in this boneyard wondering what the fuck to do with the rest of y'r life? . . . That's what frets me. I doubt y'd be laying out my flares, and the Liberty's shirt y'gave me, every Saturday night . . . Have y'guessed, old darling? . . . That's roughly what I'm doing. I don't do it . . . but it crosses my mind. . .

How in hell do I start again, Blair? . . . In the words of the old song, I've mourned my love for a year and a day. Bit longer than that, too. How do I start to find a new man now I'm facing forty, eh?

Don't want to make too much of it, Blair, but the world's very different. Having each other, we just didn't notice it changing. There's the problem . . . Out in the bars they're all trying to look twenty. Manage it too, if they keep to the shadows. Blair, I don't

want a callow teenager. I'm a carpenter, not a bloody sculptor.
I'm not out to shape anyone. . .
Let's get to the point. I've mentioned this Harry Plimsoll
character before. He still draws me. He's kicking and screaming
and scared of involvement . . . but he still draws me . . . As I've
said, we're of an age, give or take a year. That's half the problem.
Now y'call to mind how I'd tweak silver hairs from my temples?
How y'told me to give up the losing battle . . . Harry's fighting
his age. Tints his hair, I'd guess, but that's just a symptom. . .
Looking round the boneyard . . . but y'll need to do it through
my eyes . . . y'd note it's spring. I need someone to walk with
in the spring, Blair . . . We all do. Harry does . . . but he's scared
to walk with me . . . To mix it a bit, he'd need to accept a touch
of early autumn in himself, whatever the bloody season, if he
walked with me . . . I'm offering him a pleasant stroll among
the fields, knowing they'll turn to harvest. Harry can't accept
that . . . Just so long as he can look at a bit of frisky lamb, he'll
not look at me . . . I'm his shaving mirror, Blair. . .
Gordon pauses to find another cigarette. His ramblings are
suddenly forgotten. His senses dulled from an evening of
drinking alone, he's still aware enough of his surroundings to
be convinced that he's being observed.
By steadying himself against Blair's headstone, he gets up. Without caring who might be around, he treads through the marble
chippings to the foot of the grave, spreads his feet either side of
a small urn, and pisses into the grass. His zip closed again, he
draws on his cigarette and stares into the thicker darkness of a
clump of laurels. As though his cigarette's glow sent a message
that has been received and understood, a match flickers in reply.
The match is spent too soon for Gordon to make out anything
but the shape of a man of average height clothed in dark
sportswear. The figure moves with casual ease between the
headstones that are bleached, for a moment, in the moonlight.
Gordon remains motionless and mumbles softly, so that he'll
not be taken for an eccentric given to haunting a cemetery in the
early hours.
–Who've we here, Blair? . . . Seems we're about to break new
ground. Y'could be in on the start of a new phase in my life,
Blair. I'll need to manage without y'r approval this time. . .

Once the man is no more than a couple of strides away, Gordon can see he's somewhere between twenty-five and forty. He puts it down to exhaustion and whisky that he can be no more exact. There is, too, something both elusive and familiar about the sportsman that Gordon cannot pinpoint. Either rain, or a shower recently taken, has flattened the hair, and there's a waft of aftershave that Gordon remembers Blair afforded, just once, as a birthday gift.

The man steps up onto Blair's grave, levelling with Gordon, but without realising how close he's coming to a swift upper-cut. How could a stranger know he's desecrating a private shrine? Unaware of Gordon's memories, he stands running down the zip of a charcoal-grey track suit, on the very spot where earth was shovelled over Blair Brodie's coffin.

The stranger smiles with an innocence at odds with his years. The eyebrows arch so guilelessly that Gordon is disarmed. He blames himself for not moving half-way, or more, towards the laurels but this is soon forgotten as he studies a hairless chest and pectorals that have, he judges, been developed in a gym, not by manual work such as his own.

A moment later, the stranger pushes down the pants of his track suit. Gordon is bemused. Once again the man embodies contrasts. Beneath the dapper exterior, there are football shorts so used that wave on wave of ingrained sweat quite overpowers the expensive aftershave. Yet the boyish, almost virginal limbs fascinate Gordon. Whatever the man's age, the jawline is unshadowed, and there's little more than the lightest of downs on the classically rounded thighs.

Two hands are raised and placed with gentle trust on Gordon's shoulders. He notes the unscarred forearms just as the moon is lost among extensive cloud. In the darkness, Gordon begins to unbutton his shirt, allowing himself to be pulled closer as he does so. Two naked torsos exchange a natural warmth.

It is an instant in which Gordon can admit a hunger in himself that's gone unsatisfied too long. Fumbles in alleys behind the main-line railway stations, even a couple of weekends with Harry Plimsoll, have not afforded the chance for him to sate himself as he needs to do.

His fingers sink like canine teeth into the stranger's neck.

Then, as their feet slur closer through the marble chippings, he experiences a surge of nausea. The crunching beneath them suggests, to Gordon, that he's helping to grind Blair's limbs, more quickly than they should be turned, to powdery dust. By chance, the stranger touches the small of Gordon's back. He shudders, the fingers linger, and revulsion is dispelled in pleasure.

Gordon's own lips begin to feed on throat, smooth cheeks and then search hungrily towards the generous mouth.
–No kissing.
His head pulled back, Gordon stares in bewilderment. It's an odd demand, when measured against the stranger's touch that falls, welcome as sunlight, on a body that has known winter too long.
–If no kissing, what?
–Take me as you'd take a younger boy at school. Look at me. I want you to see a fifteen-year-old. You're my sixth-form hero. Use me . . . The soccer match is over. The others have gone. The changing room's ours . . . Ruffle my hair . . . Go on . . . That's better. That's why you notice me. Can you smell the soap still on me from the showers? I want you to notice it. I had my first wet dreams about you . . . Come on. Don't let's get caught. You've got your chance. Rip my shorts down. Don't worry about me . . . Stop being so bloody gentle aand master me. Come on. Don't flunk it. Spear me with it. I want you to shaft me . . . rend me . . . tear me . . . Come on, take me now. . .

Had Gordon been more sober, or his own hunger less insistent, he'd have rejected the fantasy with hysterical laughter. The warm flesh, ripe and for the plucking, ousts all objectivity. He questions nothing. Even the adroit shuffle by which the stranger changes places with him does not seem absurd. The purpose is soon clear. The man settles his feet astride, grips Blair's headstone, and drops his head so that, only by covering him, can Gordon reach forward with his lips to tease the soft nape hair and the recently washed neck.

As he thrusts forward, Gordon likens himself to a snake sloughing old skin, readying itself, as he does, for the challenge of a new season. Though he expresses no delight when his hands close on a groin sticky with excitement, he would like to confide to the night sky how much he hopes this casual encounter will do more than sate plain lust. He needs to feel in himself the stirrings of late March that will not abate when the stranger has gone.

–That's it. Impale me, tough school prefect. I've waited for you. You've ignored me. Others wanted to touch my peaches and cream skin. I've kept it for you. Hold me firmer. Delve deeper . . . Deeper still, my beach-bronzed hero. Ignore my boyish cock. There's no pleasure there for you . . . That's it, leave that to me . . . Think of your pleasure . . . Now . . . Think of yourself . . . Make it soon, now . . . Soon. . .

The man's fantasy burgeons swift as leaves on a cherry tree but Gordon hardly listens. However fleeting the moment, he is at one with all the green sap rising around him and far beyond the desolate cemetery.

–Yes . . . Make it now . . . Now . . . Now. . .

The tenderest and most considerate lovers may work for years to ensure their orgasms coincide. By one chance in however many million, it happens for these two strangers in a North London cemetery. But there, any similarity with gentle lovers ends.

No sooner has a throttled gasp faded than the man pulls free with a wrench not at all compatible with the selflessless he's just been offering. Gordon, anaesthetised to discomfort by whisky, notes the speed with which both football shorts and track suit are adjusted.

When he has combed his hair and is ready for the road, the stranger turns and extends a sticky palm. Still quite bemused, Gordon shakes it.

–Goodnight to you, my friend.

It's more than a few moments before Gordon can distance himself from what has happened. If he has used the stranger - and he concedes that he has - then, equally but in a very different way, the stranger has used him. Gordon feels he's just been playing a walk-on in the man's dream script. The sequence is over, the satisfied director has dismissed the cast, popped his own technical equipment away, and is probably off to do some more auditioning in a fresh location.

Only as the retreating figure squares his shoulders, changing once more from temporary adolescence to confident manhood, does the reason for his seeming not an entire stranger occur to

Gordon. They have met before or, to be exact, Gordon and he have been in the same company. The priggish media man, so nervous of his reputation at the gay coffee evening, and the sexy schoolboy, are one. After midnight he plays a teenager ravenous for seduction. By day he's quick to dissociate himself from Dave, the gentle bus conductor, who admitted affection for a fourteen-year-old.

With a sad shrug at yet another instance of the double standards that, to him, characterise Londoners, Gordon tucks in his shirt before pulling a last cigarette from his pack. As a breeze flusters the wet grass, he crouches by the headstone and flicks his lighter. He watches a gobbet of sperm, not his own, that has hit the marble, and is now inching down from the A of Blair to the O of Brodie.

☆

With luck on her side, Noreen calculates, she'll be in Athens in less than twelve hours, and meeting Dimitri in no more than fourteen. Given no bomb incidents at dawn, or early rush-hour pile ups on the bridge, she can expect to be changing into her new travelling suit in less than six. More immediately, she'll need to make another round of the wards within five minutes.

She slips her diary into a shoulder-bag, not so much because she expects to make many entries during the coming evenings, or because she's given to rereading her own jottings. If asked about this habit of toting an old exercise book everywhere, she'd probably laugh and say that, without it, she'd not feel properly dressed. While washing sherry dregs from the tumblers, she thinks of Harry, and even considers adding a postcript to her latest entry. If she can trace any similarity between their two characters and their very different lives, it is, she's sure, a wish to be in charge of situations instead of allowing others to shape a pattern for them. In Harry's case, this accounts for the poorly-concealed hysteria that his mother's illness has caused.

Her thoughts run on to an estimation of how far she might have skimped giving Ricky more of her free time in recent years. Had the acceptance of extra shifts, then of promotion, been simply to ensure treats for him immediately after his grandfather's death? Might there have been some element of compensating for a rejection of her half-grown son whose mouth, whose arms, even whose walk had been a reminder of her chaotic marriage to Frederick Woodward?

Noreen rinses her hands. Not for the first time, she thinks she might have been braver. Had she found, and involved herself with a Dimitri figure in London, the relationship might have been less controllable, but Ricky would have had a figure other than his grandfather as a role model. One who would be still alive. The chances of police at the door and a three months' probation would, very likely, have been less.

Impatient with all the might have beens, Noreen tries to formulate some image of her son's way of life. She hopes his grandparents' scepticism has been passed on to him, if he happens to have become entangled with young trendies in London or elsewhere. From what she'd seen of them, as occasional patients, they've seemed not so much revolutionaries as students on a long graduation party until, bored with permissiveness, they've been ready to return to stockbroking or a sinecure in public relations. Like their ideology, the cheap drugs and uninhibited sex are counters in a game in which those without a fall-black position must end as losers. She does not want Ricky to be a loser, and trusts that one skirmish with the law will have been sufficient for him to avoid the drugs trap. But sex?

Noreen remembers the sole occasion on which Ricky had called to see her at the hospital. More than one probationer had eyed him over tea, yet he'd shown no interest. Nor had he reacted, positively or negatively, when a pair of giggling male therapists had passed in the corridor, ogling the son rather than the middle-aged mother.

She pats her hair and peeks into the mirror before setting off on her two-mile round of the wards and corridors. It occurs to her that Ricky might already be settled with some girl. It's possible that, unknown to herself, she may be grandmother to an infant bawling for attention in a bedroom not ten minutes' walk away. It would be characteristic of Ricky to set up a situation that could not be undone by argument. How else had she herself behaved by as good as eloping with Bloody Woodward?

As she gently turns the handle leading to Margaret Plimsoll's room, Noreen resolves to write her son a letter, care of his grandmother. A day out, with a pub lunch, could mark the start of Ricky's understanding that she regards him as a young adult.

Margaret is quite awake. She welcomes Noreen with a perky smile.

–How nice of you to drop in, dear. Time for breakfast already? Now, a soft-boiled egg would do me fine . . . Four minutes in boiling, salty water always does the trick, don't you find? . . . I don't want to cause extra trouble, dear, but could you have a word about the tea? . . . Like luke-warm soup it's been these last two days . . . I'd willingly give a hand myself but . . . as you see. . .

–Mrs Plimsoll . . . It's the middle of the night. You're supposed to be asleep. . .

–What a strange time to come visiting. What kind of a world are we coming to? A nicely spoken woman like you having to work at night. My dear son too, of course. Not that I'd stand in his way. He's got more of my blood than John's, and we McCawdies are an independent lot.

–I'm very glad to hear it. About you being independent, I mean . . . That's what you need now. After all, you've got your pacemaker, so we should soon have you up and about.

Margaret's speculative look isn't lost on Noreen.

–But I'll never be able to look after myself again, shall I?

–Don't see why not. . .

The old woman looks away with a long sigh.

–You don't expect me to crawl round one of these supermarkets, do you? All those busy roads to cross, and I don't know what else?

–You're an intelligent old lady, and we all know that. Now you just listen. When any of us gets to your age we have to guard against giving up. . .

–Giving up? I've no intention to curling up like a leaf, let me tell you.

–I'm glad to hear that, too. Leaves don't curl all at once, do they? . . . We don't either. What you've got to watch is giving up the supermarket one week, then crossing a road the next. If you go on that way, take it from me, it'll soon be too much effort to go to the corner for your evening paper, and you'll take to your bed at home and lie there waiting to die . . . We want you to do things for yourself.

Margaret considers this silently. When she turns her head to look at Noreen again, the eyes are brimming with tears.

–You're going to take my home help away, aren't you? That's what you've been sent to tell me. . .

–Nonsense. Total nonsense . . . Now, in a few hours I'm off on holiday. . .

–Anywhere nice?

–Greece. So, before I go, I shall scribble a note for the almoner's office. We'll do everything we can to put life back to where it was for you . . . but . . . you've got to help. . .

–There's no going back, Nurse. Never be old and clumsy. No one wants you. I have Harry, of course, so I'm one of the lucky ones. Even so, it might have been better if that young policeman . . . I'm sure his name was Alastair . . . hadn't found me. If that sounds wicked, then I suppose an old folks' home it will have to be. I don't want to be a millstone round Harry's neck. . .

Noreen has heard it all before though not, as far as she can recall, in as effective a way as Margaret presents it. She recognises that the patient is clinging to the hem of her uniform, pleading with her to use whatever authority it may command, to put pressure on relatives. In this instance, on Harry.

–A millstone, Mrs Plimsoll? Nonsense. I'm sure Harry will do what he can, just as we shall but, as I said, you can't leave it all up to us. . .

–I suppose you're right. He's such a thoughtful boy. Rings me every night of his life, even from Amsterdam or San Francisco . . . You see that card with the arum lilies? . . . From my poor sister-in-law, Winnie . . . Arum lilies. Does she think I'm in a chapel of rest already? . . . When she's . . . when she's feeling well, she always says Harry won't marry while I'm alive. If I thought that was true, Nurse, I'd throw myself down the stairs outside. . . .

Ignoring the melodrama, Noreen seizes on the final phrase. . .

–How do you know there are stairs outside? Have you been walking to the door?
–How could I? . . . You won't forget about my breakfast egg being soft-boiled?
–We'll see what can be done. Now, you just concentrate on getting plenty of rest. They'll have you into the swing of things before I'm back from holiday.
–We can never go back. Have you ever been to Kenya? No? . . . I couldn't go back there. The Mau Mau's in charge now. They do tribal dances and worse on the lawns of Government House, you can be sure of that . . . Doesn't matter though. Everyone I knew is dead. John . . . Alastair. . .
–Yes. Now this Alastair . . . your cousin?

In an instant, it is as though the relationship of the two women - one a frail octoganerian, the other half her age - has been transposed. Margaret Plimsoll is no longer a bit of detritus tossed in the March winds. She is as self-assured as the Mother Superior of a girls' convent, and Noreen is in her study for a reprimand.

–Not *any* cousin, Nurse. My Highland cousin, the regimental doctor to His Majesty's Rifles in Nairobi. He encouraged my voluntary work among the poor little piccanins suffering from trachoma. It's a disease of the eyes, but then, I suppose you know that. Hundreds of them I helped . . . Of course, nowadays these television programmes make out we were all like Hitler. . .

Had this been said at the outset of their conversation, Noreen could have accepted it as the ramblings of an old and lonely person. Even a short acquaintanceship, plus a chance remark by Amanda Sopworth, lead her to think that Margaret is adept at diversionary tactics.

–I'm sure you weren't. Like Hitler, I mean. So you helped hundreds of children? You'd none of your own, had you?

Half-expecting a hard stare, and not amazed by rheumatic fingers pleating the coverlet compulsively, Noreen is somewhat startled by Margaret's laugh. It is harsh, metallic even, like something heard in a jungle.

–Got it all worked out, Nurse, haven't you? Just like Harry. Simple kindness can't be enough . . . All this Freud . . . Dear

me, I don't know what came over me. Must be these pain-killers
. . . Would you like a chocolate? They're from Harrods. Harry
brought them, needless to say. Not the sort of thing one of my
neighbours would send. . .

In the quietness of the corner room, Noreen bites into the
chocolate and savours the cognac, but she is not deflected. She's
more certain by the minute that there's something Margaret has
been concealing, maybe from herself, for a very long time.

–You enjoyed those years in Nairobi?

–Just look at me now, dear. Would you think I'd had the
chance to waltz with the Prince of Wales? Not this one, I
mean. Edward . . . Didn't bother. Nervous little creature . . .
and there were rumours no lady would repeat. No, I didn't
bother. I danced with Alastair that night . . . With John, too.
Wouldn't have done to have set tongues wagging, would
it?

–Your husband's work took him away from Nairobi now and
again?

There's quite a pause before Margaret replies. Her voice assumes
the charm of royalty pausing for a word, and then passing on
its way.

–Not all the time . . . You've been very kind to spend an hour
with me. Tell me one thing honestly before you get back to your
other duties . . . Am I going to die?

The ploy has been tried once too often. It is Noreen's turn
to laugh.

–Die? We haven't sent the padre in yet, have we? Yes, I must go
soon and you must sleep . . . Tell me, was it lonely when John
was away?

–Well, Alastair would drop in. Not too regularly, you understand?

–I think I do . . . Have you ever talked about Alastair and the old
days to Harry?

–What's it to do with him? . . . Or any of you? . . .

Quite abruptly, Margaret weeps. She throws her head from side
to side on the pillows in anguish, and gulps noisily. It is no act.
Harry might have said that the mask has fallen. Noreen, using
an image more familiar to her, compares Margaret's distress to
the lancing of a heavily infected boil.

—What's all this about, Margaret? Whatever happened, it was more than forty years ago. . .
—Not for me, it's not. Why did he let me marry John? . . . I could have been happy with him. Who needed a Prince of Wales in a little cocked hat? . . . Alastair was my Prince of Hearts. . .
—Only one more question, Margaret. It's better answered, you know. No sense in lying there and having it trouble you like an infection. . .
—I don't know the answer. Even the colour of Harry's hair, before he started touching it up, couldn't tell me. John's hair went Alastair-colour in the summer as well, you see. I can't be sure, Nurse, which of them is Harry's father. . .
—Harry was born in England, surely?
—Alastair insisted I came home for the baby. I always said he was a bit premature. Harry, I mean . . . Alastair wrote from time to time. Care of the Post Office, of course . . . I never replied. Just hoped he'd come home, too. But we heard he'd married a coffee planter's daughter. He's been dead ten years now . . . Do you wonder I hate Kenya and the Mau Mau? . . . They're all dead. John . . . Alastair . . . Winnie might as well be . . . And now there's no one left to call me Margaret.
—What does Harry call you?
—Him? . . . Well, naturally, he calls me Mother . . . Tell me, you nurses have to swear that oath, just like the doctors, don't you?
—If you're worried I'll repeat any of this to Harry, calm down.
—He'd reject me. That's the word, isn't it? I'm sure he would. He'd put me in one of those dreadful places I've read about. I'd have to have what's left of my hair clubbed, even if they let me keep my own clothes. They chop off your hair to avoid the lice . . . You won't tell him, will you? You wouldn't have it on your conscience that you'd helped put me away?
—Margaret! Yes, I'm going to call you that. Margaret, there's no need to tear my heart out. I do have a mother of my own. And I have a son. This is 1970. Stop inventing the future. It's not going to be something out of a Hitchcock horror, and I'll hear no more of it. Quite time to turn out this light so you can sleep. . .
—No, dear. Leave the light. It'll be dark enough in the grave. . .
—Margaret! Let's have a little less about graves and a bit more about living. When I'm back from Greece we'll have some tea

together. Not here. In your flat. You'll make it and I'll drink it. One last word. Your hair looks very nice . . . unclubbed. Don't worry about what happened forty years ago, eh? . . . Sleep comfortably.

☆

The repeated ringing of a bell wakes Harry at last though he's slept for barely an hour. His first thought, as he drags on his dressing gown and lurches to the stairs, is that he really can't put off having a phone extension in his bedroom much longer. His second is that Paul Harding must have been more drunk than he'd sounded. What other reason can there be for a second phone call? The regrets, apologies and explanations had all been given and accepted. The conversation ended with Harry's promise that he'd not cancel his ticket, merely negotiate a later flight.

It's not until he reaches the landing outside the kitchen that he realises it's the front door-bell that's woken him. He curses his own stupidity in switching on a light. Its glow will filter through the fanlight over the street door and he'll not be able to check on his after-midnight caller. He's wrecked his own custom of squinting through the lounge curtains to check on whoever's arrived without prior arrangement.

He dallies a moment on the landing. If it's Gordon on the doorstep he'll receive a terse rejection, whatever the time or weather. Gordon is a long-term planner. The mere thought of him conjures up, for Harry, a hell of pushing a supermarket trolley round the Elephant and Castle Shopping Centre every Saturday afternoon. As for Gordon watching at the gate while the soup grows cold but still ready to sympathise with any invented excuse, that's a situation Harry cannot bear to think about.

Since he can see nothing of the caller through the frosted door panels, Harry eases back the bolt and unhooks the chain with an ember of hope. There's an outside chance it could be a special messenger from the hospital. By the rarest of flukes, Margaret's pacemaker might have failed.

Just inside the open gate, Fred stands balancing the window-box on his head. The faulty street lamp strobes his grin so that he resembles a performer in a cabaret.
–Hi, Harry . . . Guessed you'd still be about. . .
–You weren't expected. I've got to be up early, and I was asleep. What is it?
–Brought you a prezzie . . . Going to ask me in?
–When I need a window-box I'll buy one. I told you, I was asleep. . .
–That all? . . . If you won't ask me in, I'll have to squat here till one of the others comes home.

As he speaks, Fred removes the window-box from his head, upends it, and sits astride it as though perching on a street bollard. Harry's torn. He glimpses the healthy, untired flesh that shows above an open shirt. His annoyance at Fred's cheek in supposing he can return when he wills is equal to his lust - but only for a milli-second. Fred tips the balance with a conspiratorial wink. Harry checks his enthusiasm before he replies. There'll be a price tag on Fred's gift. He intends to discover what it is.

–Right. You can come in. Let's be clear about one thing. If you want to stay, you sleep on the couch in the lounge . . . It's a communal lounge. Let's hope the bouncer hasn't brought anyone back.

Fred's already over the doorstep and giving Harry's shoulder a friendly squeeze with his free hand.
–Right, Harry. Wouldn't want to start the bouncer growling. I'll creep up, just in case the copper downstairs is about. Don't need him towering over me, do I? . . . Hope you haven't forgotten the name's Fred.

There's something about Fred's whispered banter that makes Harry uneasy. Confident by the end of his first visit, he now seems to think of himself as a long-standing ally.

They make directly for the lounge. Fred drops onto the couch and removes his shoes while Harry is closing the curtains.
–Look, Fred. The truth is sometimes brutal, but it's best. I don't go looking for presents from anyone . . . especially from someone who just happened to come back on a stormy night. . .

—When's the last time anyone gave you anything, Harry?
—What's that to do with it?
—No need to get snappy. I got the answer.
—Good on the psychology as well, eh? . . . I'll get a blanket.
Harry begins to amble from the windows, but Fred is quicker. He blocks Harry at the door and kisses him full on the lips.
—Are you mad? Any moment someone could. . .
—Not a chance, Harry.
He kisses Harry again, at the base of the throat.
—Don't you understand? The bouncer. . .
—Just murdered him, Harry, with a couple of kisses. No point in staring out there. No one's on the landing . . . well, your conscience maybe. . .
—What're you after, Fred?
—Well, a room – something like the bouncer's might be a start.
—Nothing doing. Blethering about murdering my neighbour with kisses. Have you been taking drugs?
—Never use 'em.
—So you say. You'd need to talk to the landlord about a room. He's got other houses. But he's out of town. . .
Fred's eyes twinkle as he allows Harry to pass to a cupboard on the landing. Feeling he shouldn't throw his ace too early, Fred decides he'll not press Harry on his status in the house. Not as he's carrying back a blanket and a pillow.
—Bet I can guess what you're thinking right now, Harry. You reckon I'm here with a hard-luck story, eh? Brought the window-box as a sweetener, that's what you reckon, don't you?
—No one's tried a window-box before, I'll give you that. . .
—Told you I'd get a job, didn't I? . . . I can get bulbs, too. There's sheds stuffed with 'em. Hyacinths . . . iris . . . gladioli. That back yard would look a treat. . .
—Not much of an expert yet, are you? There's an ash tree over the yard, in case you hadn't noticed. An ash kills anything under it. . .
—No problem. Soon bump it out with a can of acid and bugger the conservation freaks. . .
—When all the tenants here need a gardener, I'll bear you in mind. . .

Once more, Fred is tempted but, as before, he uses Harry's trick of changing the subject.
–Look, Harry. I know you're tired. I'm not asking for coffee or anything. Just give me a minute to explain. About needing a room, I mean. It's this way, see? I'm pissed off with hostels. Bet you've never needed to try them. I can't stand it much more. . .
–Thought you were in some bed and breakfast place near King's Cross? I'm tired, Fred. Don't give me fantasies. . .
–All right. I told you I had to get out, didn't I? . . . I was in a hostel before, and I've had to book in again. But I don't want it, Harry. Dormitories stinking with meths drinkers yelling and farting all night. Look, I know I look like I've got straw behind my ears. I'm nearly twenty-four, for Christ's sake. I mean, how'd you like it if shitty old hands tried to grope your balls every time you made for the shower? Doesn't turn me on, that's for sure. . .
–So?
–So, I'm for out. The wages over the park . . . calm down, Harry Honey Bear, not that park by the corner . . . the wages aren't bad. Problem is, landlords want to grab your whole bloody pay packet, most of it anyway, for their crummy rooms. Come on, Harry, couldn't you do something about the bouncer's room?
–He's been here as long as I have. What do I know about you? If we let you in, who's to say you haven't got some girl in the family way? Next thing we know you'd be rearing a family here, with washing all round the kitchen. . .
–Good with the words, aren't you? There again, you would be . . . journalist and all that. Harry, do I spell it out? . . . After last time you should know. I'm gay. Like you. . .
–Who's to say you won't be bringing blokes back for cash, when you run short in the middle of the week?
–If I didn't fancy you, I'd thump you for that. I'm not rent. Never would be. Anyway, what's this landlord think about all your casual pick-ups? Who's to say I haven't been watching you off and on down the coffee stall? Taking a risk with the landlord's furniture you are, I'd say. Not to speak of that set of coronation mugs behind you. They'd fetch a bit down the old Portobello.
–I hope you're no risk. . .

–Me? You couldn't be more wrong, Harry Honey Bear. *I'm* taking the risk. You could have a regular upstairs. I'm not into threesomes, as it happens.
–You won't get the chance. You're on the couch. It's what you *are* into that's keeping me from my bed.
Harry yawns, a bit obviously. He lifts his wrist before realising he's left his watch on the bedside table. For Fred, it's time to throw his trump cards. In the words of his grandfather – but only in the privacy of his allotment – it's a shit or bust move.
–Me? I'm into having a bit of fun. No point in calling yourself gay if you're not, is there? Half of the blokes I see around look as gay as a bloody carnival in the Arctic . . . You asked, and I'll tell you. I'm into being around with a bloke I can feel relaxed with, have a giggle with, go out with and do simple things when there's a bit of cash about. That's what I'm into. And one thing, before you start your sparring with long words, I know the bloke I want to share these things with. Take it from me, I don't give up easily.
–Nice for you both.
Harry's swift answer is all he can think of to gain time. Fred runs his hands through his hair but Harry has barely a chance to do anything but note that there seems to be, by the soft glow of the wall lights, more dark honey than chestnut in the curls. Fred has closed in to confront him face to face.
–Glad you approve. Nice for both of us, old Honey Bear, I'd have said.
–What's all this Honey Bear nonsense? D'you think I'm having you, or Gordon Laird, or any other bugger moving in here and restricting my life?
–Who's Gordon Laird?
–Forget him. Well, do you?
–What you so nervous about, Mr Landlord? I can pay my way. And don't bother acting all amazed. I was here earlier, waiting for you. . .
–I don't want anyone waiting for me. Or checking up on me. . .
–Will you bloody listen? Grandpa downstairs was never a copper, unless he's a stilt-walker too . . . As for the bouncer, if the bugger won't lie down, I'll kill him with a third kiss.
And Fred does so. As if it is the most natural thing in the world for him to be doing, he begins to stroke Harry's chest – until

his hand is knocked angrily aside. His self-protective myth shattered, his opponent equipped with maybe more facts that could be used against him, Harry skips from the debris as nimbly as a cornered politician.

–This is bloody ridiculous, Fred. You come round here when I'm still half-asleep. You pretend all you want is a room. All you want is a few evening classes in growing up . . . and probably a career guidance officer thrown in. In return for what? A bit of slap and tickle I can get any night of the week. Without strings.

–Well tried, Harry. You're on a loser, but well tried. Same as the rest of us, you need company like we all need beer and chips. Just too proud to admit it. . .

–All this psychology! You could go far. Not as far as I might be going. Thinking of following me to Australia? I've got a ticket, for one, on that table. . .

–That desperate, were you? . . . Tickets can be cashed in. Right now, I'd say the farthest you ought to be going is your bed. Could do with some kip myself. I've got a job to go to in the morning, even if you haven't. . .

Although he's careful to hide it, Fred's astounded that this doesn't provoke an outburst about making decisions for other people in their own homes. Harry complies with the suggestion only because another few hours' sleep will defer any need for decisive action. He interprets Fred's private smile as gratitude for being allowed even a temporary toe-hold in the flat.

–You needn't lie there with dreams of a first romance, either. I've always steered well clear of emotional virgins, Fred, so don't build up any hopes. In the flat's one thing; in my bed's another. We'll have to talk in the morning. . .

–Need to be early. I'm off at half seven. Just remember one thing, Honey Bear. I never had anyone worth coming home for till now, see? Think about it. If that doesn't tire you out, ask yourself when you last did, too. Happy dreams.

The questions linger in Harry's mind only for the few minutes it takes him to reach his room and fall, still wrapped in his dressing gown, onto the duvet. Those few minutes are enough for him to admit to himself that Fred's guess has hit its mark. Who has there been since the three years shared with Gwyn more than twenty years previously? A succession of weekends, shared holidays, and abortive beginnings. As his arm stretches across the empty half of the divan, he wonders if he should call to Fred. He decides it is too late: perhaps in a larger sense.

On the couch, Fred props himself among some cushions, unfolds the sheets of paper he's cadged at Waterloo, taps the stem of his biro on his teeth, and thinks how best to begin his letter.

It's already gone nine in the morning before Harry opens the lounge door. Cushions, pillow and blanket are ranged neatly, and Fred has left. Harry goes to check the kitchen. The window is open to the cold dry morning, and the window-box is in place. By one corner of the table there's a sheet of toilet paper on which Fred has printed *See You Soon Honey Bear*.

Harry scrunches the note into a ball and hurls it over the garden fence so that it lands among his neighbour's daffodils. He turns in irritation, and fills the kettle with such impatience that cold water sprays onto his naked chest and trickles down his belly. The effect on him is no different from that produced by the unexpected touch of Fred's cool fingers. He has an instant erection.

☆

One hour's delay in the flight departure isn't something Noreen has been anticipating yet she's not altogether amazed. Her morning, once clear of the hospital, has seemed almost too smooth. Rain clouds that have hung over London with scarcely a break for days and nights have cleared. Her wait on dry pavements before a bus nosed from under the railway bridge at Waterloo was seconds, not minutes. Neither burst water mains nor lorries shedding their loads impeded progress to Piccadilly. At Hounslow West, there was another bus ready to ferry her to Heathrow. Having expected to take a taxi, she now has a bit of extra cash for the gifts she intends to pick up in one of the ever-growing number of boutiques that surrounded the island's harbour. So the announcement of a delay doesn't panic her.

A present for her mother has never been a problem. It is more difficult each year, Noreen finds, to think of something for her son. She's sure Dimitri, with his common sense, will suggest she keeps her eyes open for what others of Ricky's age are buying. It will be easy to spot the first-timers. They'll be snatching up cheap miniatures of windmills and ruins, or mass-produced casts of ancient gods and heroes.

Settled with another cup of coffee, she's about to while away the hour with a collection of short stories, when her fingers touch Ricky's letter in her shoulder-bag. Having grabbed it in the hospital's reception area on her way out, she's given it little thought. Even in the tube, as she'd checked through her passport, tickets and travellers' cheques, she'd done no more than smile at the coincidence of its arrival. Had it not been delivered at some impossibly early hour, and by hand, she'd have had to wait a fortnight before reading it.

She takes a first sip of coffee, eases up a bit of stamp-edging which seals the pages, and settles back to catch up with news she expected to enjoy high above the Swiss Alps.

A film of cream rises and settles on her neglected coffee. Her eyes, moving ever more quickly, race through the second page down to the love and kisses. She looks up and, for some minutes stares ahead, oblivious to other passengers who pass close to her, singly, or in family groups, or in pairs. Still gripping the letter, she asks a neighbouring couple to guard her luggage while she weaves among the crowded benches of the transit lounge to a cigarette kiosk.

A nod of thanks to her neighbours, and she resettles herself, lights a cigarette, and rereads her son's letter, evaluating every phrase.

It could be worse. Noreen accepts that this first reaction is negative, but it's the one that recurs again and again long after she's folded the pages into their original creases. The letter might have confirmed just what had worried her hours earlier. There could have been a girl, perhaps a babe as well, who'd weigh Ricky down for years to come. She knows it's unfair to ignore the man's responsibility in such situations. Then she sighs and stubs her cigarette, while brushing justice aside as something more suited to cool and unemotional moments.

Useless to pretend she's cool and unemotional. Noreen knows

that. At least, she thinks, snatching at any positive reaction, Ricky should still be able to enjoy some of the leisure and some of the chances to travel that she herself was denied by too hasty a marriage. Yet why should he be so coy about this man he seems so keen to get involved with? Having had the courage to tell his mother he finds himself more at ease with a man than with a woman, why not tell more? She can only conclude that this is another example of her son's insistence on his own private space. It is as though the letter opens a door just wide enough for her to see Ricky as an independent adult, but not sufficiently wide for her to catch more than a glimpse of some nameless outline standing by him.

That Ricky has elected to live with man older than himself neither startles nor disgusts her. She's long since given up being amazed at the nearest and dearest who've appeared at her patients' bedsides. As to what people prefer to do in the quiet security of their own bedrooms, she views that as their business. As a nurse, she does hope that giving each other pleasure will not entail arriving on the hospital doorstep with broken limbs, or still welded to some of the bizarre accessories that are joked about in staff canteens.

She lights another cigarette and glances at the flight indicator. Boarding will begin in another fifteen minutes. Noreen is not given to dramatic gestures. She doesn't even consider phoning Dimitri and telling him she must return to Central London to cope with a family crisis. This doesn't preclude a growing wish to make some contact with Ricky, letting him know he shouldn't worry, but that she feels they should sit down together and talk.

This presumes, she doesn't need reminding, that Ricky will agree there's anything to talk about. There'll be no question of persuading him to wait awhile . . . Would he arrive alone, or with this man who has stepped into his life?

After a little thought, Noreen decides it's possible an older man might bring Ricky's nomadic days to an end. Presumably Mr Right has some kind of a career and, unless he's a hopeless romantic, is unlikely to agree to them moving around the country like a couple of gypsies. And Ricky? One thing will have been learned from his own wanderings, she's sure. Her son won't be flattered by candle-lit dinners, or even the reflected glory of being seen with a well-known face or name. He'll never be any man's shadow.

Knowing she's being uselessly protective, Noreen has one underlying doubt. It's possible the older man might be more skilled in playing Ricky along. The mountie did it. What would Mr Right see in Ricky after ten years, without a mortgage or kids to encourage them to keep trying?

Suddenly Noreen begins to giggle. It's near hysteria, but she doesn't care. What has kept her and Dimitri together? True, there've not been the challenges of everyday living. Ricky will have to meet them.

She blows her nose, checks the change in her purse, gathers her hand luggage and makes for the phone. Whatever happens in ten years can look after itself, she decides.

Listening to the distant sound of her mother's telephone ringing, Noreen hopes Ricky hasn't contacted his grandmother lately. It will increase the chances that he'll be dropping in soon, or at least phoning. Indirect contact is a poor substitute but Noreen feels it imperative that he should know his letter's been read and that nothing in it alters her love for him.

After three minutes, Noreen presumes her mother has taken advantage of the fine morning to shop in her local street market. She replaces the receiver, checks her watch, and estimates she has just about time to send Ricky a card, care of his grandmother. Grabbing a black and white reproduction of Byron's statue in Hyde Park, she scribbles O.K. three times, signs it, and adds a postscript sending love to all. She's certain Ricky will interpret the last word as she intends. She posts the card and hurries towards the departure gate.

Fumbling for her boarding pass, she wonders how much her mother might be able to glean, in her joking way, about Ricky's whereabouts. His letter was quite clear. He intends moving in with Mr Right. If anything further can be learned, Noreen trusts her mother to discover it. *Love to all*, when there are only two of them, must alert her to some development.

Old Rita Humby continues to stare at the telephone long after it has stopped ringing. She does not see it, nor has she heard the bell. Her features contorted into a pantomime grin, she lies, like a huge discarded doll, in one corner of her lounge. A Wedgewood flower pot holder remains in her lap, but the begonia rex has tumbled onto the carpet. It rests between her knees, unnaturally watered by a lengthening stream of urine.

☆

Nervous tension manifests itself in Harry as it always has done. He spends much of the morning alternating between countless mugs of coffee and visiting the lavatory. By lunch-time he is still no nearer a solution. The problem is not whether he should let Fred into his house or his bed. Of far deeper concern to Harry is whether he wishes to risk letting a twenty-three-year-old, or any man at all, into his life.

Since he doesn't doubt that Fred will turn up again, quite unpredictably, within hours, Harry begins to plan a sensible, unemotional chat. Over a beer, he'll suggest it's far too early for Fred to think of settling. Fred should give himself a fair chance by mixing with younger men, joining a progressive campaign or two, even a political party, maybe seeing how he could get on with others in a commune. It might be best not to close the door too firmly, Harry feels, for their one night together was enjoyable. They might meet for a drink; not too often. It would need to be agreed that there should be no sort of commitment between them. All that could be gone into in say, five or six years.

This seems very valid until, a little after two o'clock, Harry is pulling the lavatory chain for the umpteenth time. It then occurs to him that in five or six years' time he'll feel even less like having an upheaval in his life. Fred's energy won't have diminished, and the independence in both of them is likely to be more marked than it is at present.

As to Fred being too young to nest, one glance through the bathroom window demolishes that approach. On such a March afternoon, Harry – five years younger than Fred at the time – discussed setting up house with Gwyn.

So the problem's still unresolved as Harry pulls on his duffel coat and joins those who are also free to do so in a walk along the Clapham Road on the first sunny afternoon of the year. From time to time, he diverts himself by pausing in front of some of the many old houses that are being renovated. Whether the young workmen, stripped to their jeans, take him for an architect studying façades, he neither knows nor cares. Once in Clapham, he meanders from shop to shop, idly curious about restaurant menus, and a little more interested in the old second-hand shops that are giving place to showrooms of antiques.

He wanders on until he notes with pleasure that the cafeteria on the Common is open. Before he's ready to lose himself among the little crowd that's beginning to occupy tables on the sunny side of the building, he knows he'll need to make for the underground toilet.

It's not until he's washing his hands that Harry notices that the spring warmth has led to increased activity below, as well as above ground. There are whispers and rustlings behind him. He glances in the mirror and is so transfixed that a good five minutes pass before he leaves.

The doors of all eight cubicles to the rear of the toilet are open. Across the marbled floor between them – the four to the right and the four to the left – a stately fancy dress dance is in progress. A Nazi officer with monocle, rouged cheeks and open greatcoat emerges. He's not alone for too long. A younger figure, wearing a surplice brief as a child's petticoat, yet otherwise naked, prances from another cubicle, still adjusting an improvised mitre. The couple survey each other briefly, then disappear into what Harry terms the Nazi's bolt-hole. For a moment, the trysting place is deserted. Soon enough, a man of fifty creeps from the shadows. He's naked, apart from a schoolboy's cap and scarf. He sidles noiselessly towards the bolt-hole and is enthralled by what he sees, until the door is slammed. When he retreats, Harry is in his line of vision but the schoolboy takes no interest in the onlooker.

At last a partner for him appears from the last doorway on the left. A little person in a black wet-suit shuffles across the marble. Difficult to say much more of this one, other than to note that only his eyes are visible. His head is encased in black leather.

Small as he is, he's strong enough to drag the schoolboy - unless the schoolboy is merely pretending reluctance. The little man is like an executioner, Harry thinks. This time the pair have gone not to a bolt-hole but to a condemned cell.

Quite shaken, Harry moves very slowly up the steps. I am all of them, he murmurs to himself. I am Nazi, bishop, schoolboy, executioner, and all the others who have not appeared. I could play them all, maybe I do, but I wish to play none. As he steps out of the shadows, Harry asks himself what Fred might cast him as? A bishop-confessor? There's a little evidence. A schoolboy wouldn't interest Fred. A Nazi, then? Harry's seen to much backbone in Fred to think he might relish subjugation. As for playing executioner, Harry has more fear that it is Fred who might unwittingly accept that role, chopping and chopping away at an independence cherished for so long.

A cyclist has just dismounted on the pavement to Harry's right. He sees little of the man's face but hopes it will be young, placid and undemanding. He's prepared to take that on trust, while he concentrates his interest on the man's thighs which appear far healthier than the usual slabs of frozen chicken flesh to be seen during the rush hours.

The cyclist is also heading for the cafeteria. Harry follows. Just as he hopes, the man carries his tea and cake to the last empty table. Has he any objection to Harry sitting in the chair opposite? None.

–We could do with a few more afternoons like this, eh?

At least this opening gambit doesn't result in the cyclist moving hastily elsewhere. Harry has encountered neurotics so terrified by an innocent conversation that they cut and run if asked the time of day.

The cyclist nods and swallows a piece of cake.

–You might want some. I could do without any more like this. The sunshine's the only good thing about it.

Your luck, Harry thinks, may be changing. There's a simple gentleness about the features that urges him on.

–Nice place, the Common. Not far for me, either . . . You from round here?

There's a hesitation. The cyclist appears about to speak but then grows wary. Then he coughs nervously.

–Look, mate. I know it's a cheek, like . . . Could I pinch one of your fags? Might calm me down a bit.

The pack is pushed across. Harry supposes this might be an occasion on which there'll be no personal conversation. Attraction will be left unstated. They'll both agree on the old code of two strangers drifting towards a bedroom while still discussing the weather, the local football teams, or the rising price of chips.

–What's upset you?

–Nice of you to ask . . . The name's Dave . . . Not a lot anyone can do, really . . . Got to get out of my room. That's about it.

–It's happening all the time, Dave. Bloody landlords don't realise we're human beings, do they?

The cyclist says nothing while he finishes his cake. Then he leans forward so that he'll not be overheard at the neighbouring tables.

–Didn't catch your name, mate. . .

–Harry.

–Right . . . Well, Harry, it's the old cow downstairs. She's the problem, see? Threatened to call the law unless I go. Wants the room for her daughter. I know that.

–The law? What're you up to? Running a brothel or something?

–Long story, Harry. Long story. . .

–Women? . . . Men?

–She's got no evidence, see? It's all in her stinking mind . . . Know what? I reckon she's jealous. She's got no one, unless she gets her daughter round, has she? She's jealous. Sees how happy the pair of us are when we get back from a day out on the bikes. . .

Harry becomes more interested. As he stubs a cigarette into the turf, his eyes linger on the well-turned calves.

–What's it to do with her what you get up to, Dave? You're both grown men, I take it?

–That's the point, Harry. He's not . . . Hey, you're not from the law?

Harry laughs and shakes his head. Dave takes a second cigarette without asking.

–Young Sean can't hide his happiness too well, see? I've had to, for years . . . It's like this, Harry. I'm the first person who's ever taken any interest in him. I mean him, Sean, not what the old cow thinks.

–Where's his parents?

–His dad's probably inside again. His mum gives out she's a widow. I go along with that, for Sean's sake. He's got another eighteen months at school yet . . . Reckon his mum suspects how we feel about each other . . . Don't think she minds. Can't be a father to him as well, can she? Stands to reason.

Dave's directness and vulnerability astound Harry. It irks him, of course, that so muscular and appetising a body is being wasted on idealism and a fourteen-year-old. Nevertheless, the conversation prevents Harry addressing his own dilemma. When Dave suggests they leave the cafeteria and make for a bench in the sun, Harry agrees. He falls behind to retie his shoe lace. It gives him another chance to watch the play of light and shade on Dave's thighs. He catches up and they stroll without speaking. Harry's thoughts return to his own predicament. Either he must, like a cornered trickster, make a swift exit to Heathrow, or he must come to terms with Fred. If Fred could have Dave's body, and Dave could have Fred's saucy vitality, the combination might be worth a higher price than Harry's paid for years. As it is, he finds Dave fanciable, but rather less stimulating than a crossword puzzle.

They're no sooner seated than Dave turns to scrutinise Harry's face with all the desperation of a socialist lost at a hunt ball.

–Listen. Harry . . . am I talking to another? What I mean is, have you got a boy?

–I'm trying to get rid of one. Not that he's strictly a boy. Twenty-three. . .

–Get rid of him? . . . Whatever for? At least you're legal . . . Doesn't being with him make you happy?

–Well, whatever happiness is . . . yes. But I like my freedom. . .

–Make him sound like some nagging wife, you do.

–He'll not get the chance. . .

–So, where's the problem? He doesn't seem to do much to cheer you up . . . Listen. Tell you what makes my day. I'm on the way home, see? Suddenly, it's like the sun coming out. I know we're going to knock up a bite to eat together, then we'll be off on our bikes . . . If the weather's not too good, we'll choose programmes to watch. Always argue about that, we do. Ends up with a laugh, though . . . It's being with him that's important. Same for Sean, or so he says . . . It's not like that dirty old cow thinks. When the bedroom stuff happens, it'll happen . . . If you ask me, Harry, you only get obsessed with all that lark if you haven't got anything else going. That's how I see it, anyway.

What Harry's heard is, in so many respects, only a restatement of the way in which he approached his affair with Gwyn. For both of them it was a first experience of being cared about as a person. And it was so when Harry nerved himself to try again, years later, with Derek. Now, as he sits watching the distant traffic pass to and from the western suburbs, Harry wonders if he could survive the anguish of separation a third time. He remembers his feeling of disablement, as though a limb was severed. The bleeding continued, almost obliterating the pleasures.

–Think I'm obsessed with sex, Dave?

–Never said that, did I? . . . What I'm saying is, unless you're turned on in every way, it's useless. I mean, where d'you end up otherwise? Hanging round toilets, as far as I can see.

–Come on! How can you invest . . . how can you put so much of yourself on the line, Dave? I mean, this Sean, won't he grow up? Give it ten years. If he abandons you, you'll be touching forty, won't you?

–Can't cross bridges till you get to them, can you? . . . Tell you one thing, you won't find me in the toilets. What's the difference between one cock and another? Like I said, it's being with Sean that keeps me happy. I don't feel complete like, unless he's around.

–Well, you haven't got much going for you, Dave. At least you've got optimism. . .

–Thanks. You could do with a bit yourself . . . I'll need to get moving. Thanks for the fags. . .

–Have the other two. Go on. Have them.

–Thanks again. Sean and I'll work something out . . . Don't sit too long, Harry. Wouldn't want to come back in ten years and find you still here like some lonely old pensioner.

–Thank you very much. I shall only be in my late forties . . . or thereabouts.

☆

–Don't tell me . . . No prompting . . . Just sit yourself down while I gather my wits about me . . . That's fine. Lovely view, isn't it, with the sun on the water? . . . Right. Let me guess . . . We can play Twenty Questions, can't we? . . . If I can't work out who you are, that'll be it. It will, you know. They'll say the memory's gone, and have me certified as gaga in two shakes of a monkey's tail . . . No use raising your eyebrows. They'd do it. . .

Now. First guess . . . Well, I know who you're not. The chiropodist came yesterday . . . Maybe it was the day before . . . Can't say I envied him, either. At my age, the toenails are like stag's horns, they really are. . .

–You're right enough there, Mrs Plimsoll. I mean, I'm not the chiropodist. Do you really want to go on?

–Of course I do. I love a game. Put it down to this splendid afternoon if you like, but I feel quite perky . . . Could do with a cup of tea . . . We'll get one for you. I bribe the nurses with a chocolate now and again. Poor things can't afford much on their wages . . . And they've been so good to me as well . . . Tell you what I think . . . Nothing official yet. I think they'll be getting me up and about tomorrow. So . . . I just wonder. Would you be one of the doctors come to tell me about that? On second thoughts, I'd say you're not. Only my local doctor wears his street clothes when he finds time to visit me . . . which isn't often. If you were a doctor you'd wear a white coat. Yes?

–Right enough. I'm no doctor. . .

Margaret claps her hands and then waves both above her head as though claiming a Bingo prize.

–Got it . . . Well, a clue anyway. Your accent. You're a fellow Scot . . . Let's think. Some Highland relative I've forgotten about? . . . Someone I last saw as a babe, I wonder? . . . There's always the chance you're the son of a man I knew in Kenya, but your mother must have had black hair.

Gordon laughs and shakes his head before carrying the chair nearer Margaret's bedside.
—'fraid not. You're right, I'm a Scot. We met no more than six weeks ago. Your son Harry brought me to lunch one Sunday.
—He did? . . . So he did! It comes back to me. We talked about food, didn't we? You'd a friend . . . wait a tick . . . that's it. You'd a friend who was good on cooking, too . . . That's it. We talked about making a decent broth. . .
—And about porridge. . .
—Served as it should be with salt! None of this Sassenach nonsense of treacle and cream . . . My poor Harry looked quite out of it all, didn't he?
—I didn't notice. We stayed quite late, though. D'you remember we made drop scones together on your griddle? Reminded me of my mother's kitchen years ago.
Margaret's eyes moisten a little. It's the reference to childhood. Her glance lights on the present Gordon has brought.
—It was kind of you to bring me flowers. We must find a space for them. Harry sends so many. Did you choose them?
—I'm not so good on flowers, Mrs Plimsoll. I took what they had left. I thought white would brighten a hospital room. You've not forgotten I'm Gordon?
—How could I? . . . Such pretty flowers. They're called narcissus, Gordon.
—I expect your own garden could do with a tidy up, Mrs Plimsoll.
Margaret looks at him over the blooms. She smiles and Gordon thinks her attention has strayed to that large garden he glimpsed on a February afternoon.
—It'll just have to wait until Harry has a moment, I suppose. If he drops in this afternoon, we'll give him a gentle hint, shall we? . . . He's so busy, you know, I hardly like to ask. If I knew someone. . .
—I'd do what I could, Mrs Plimsoll. That is, if you wrapped up well, when you get home, I mean, you could direct and I could get cracking among the weeds, if you like. . .
—What a kind boy you are. It's almost as if I had a second son. We wouldn't want Harry to be jealous, would we?
Quite unpredictably to Gordon, Margaret becomes very silent. It

has crossed her mind that this visitor might not be all he seems. Gordon he may be, but what does he do for a living? Margaret has heard of muggers who've posed as men from the town hall in order to gain access. She feels it's time to ascertain whether he might have some connection with homes for the elderly.

–What did you say you do for a living, Gordon?

–Don't you recall that I offered to make you a pair of fitted cupboards to house all that china of yours, Mrs Plimsoll?

–So you did, dear. Help yourself to a chocolate. From Harry, of course. Too busy to bring them. Let's hope he put them on his account at Harrods, not mine. That's a bit naughty, isn't it?

With the wink and a giggle of a conspirator, Margaret also selects a chocolate. She spreads her hands on the coverlet in an expansive gesture and chews slowly, shaking her head occasionally as though considering a problem.

–Harry is being so difficult about the future. Family has always meant so much to him, Gordon. He takes after John, my husband . . . Harry's all for giving notice to that downstairs tenant of his. . .

–Tenant?

–Yes, dear. A rather dreadful old person. Know what he told me on the telephone once? I think I know you well enough to repeat it. He said I should remember, at my age, to change my underwear once a fortnight and make sure I washed my privates once a week. Coarse old creature . . . Well, as I said, Harry's all for getting him out and moving me in so I'll not be on my own if . . . if anything else should happen. What do you think, Gordon?

–I'd say that's a fine idea. You're sure Harry can do that? . . . I thought he'd only that room at the top. . .

–Now that's another question. I couldn't manage the stairs, of course. And it wouldn't do to have me pushing into Harry's private life, would it . . . You've spoken to him about the room at the top?

–No, I haven't. I did wonder about it, but there didn't seem much point. That night-club commissionaire's been living there some time. . .

Margaret stares at Gordon. She doesn't reply immediately. It takes time for her to hook a shred of toffee from under her top dentures.

–Can't say I've ever spoken to the man, Gordon: Shouldn't be much of a problem getting him out. The area's changing. Neither of Harry's tenants really fit in any more, if you see what I mean. . .

–I'd not realised Harry had the whole house, Mrs Plimsoll.

As Gordon tries to assess the startling revelations about Harry, Margaret studies his face and thinks back over their conversation. If he reminds her of anyone, it is of her late husband. She's sure that Gordon, like John more than Harry, is seeking life in the context of a family. If he can achieve this then, she suspects, he'd concede almost anything to maintain it.

–Harry never reveals too much of himself at first, Gordon. Not to anyone. He's probably been weighing you up, you know.

–I'll be honest with you, Mrs Plimsoll. . .

–Let's make it Margaret. You and I are going to be seeing each other again. More than once, I'd say.

–Well, that's good to hear, Margaret. As I was saying, well, I was going to say, I still have hopes that Harry and I might make, well, a good team.

–My generation would have said travelling companions . . . it comes to the same thing, but it sounds nicer, don't you think?

Gordon reddens a little but he's determined not to falter or look away.

–I see you understand. D'you think I should talk to Harry again? About the room at the top, at least?

–Leave that a little while. He's been so upset. I mean, I couldn't help being ill just when he was off on a month's trip to . . . wherever it was. . .

–He told me Australia.

–Did he? Then I expect that was it . . . I wouldn't expect you to shop for me, if you were upstairs with Harry, and I was downstairs. And never think I'd be waiting for you to bring me down an extra portion of roast duck, or syllabub, if you were holding a private dinner party upstairs. It wouldn't be like that at all. I do love syllabub, don't you?

–Can't say I've ever had it. Look, Margaret, I must be off soon. I was thinking of dropping round to Harry's on the off-chance, since I'm in this part of town.

–Why not? Why not? . . . If you miss him, I'll tell him you've

called. How long would you say it'll take you to walk round there?
—Fifteen minutes? I don't know the quick cuts through, you see. . .
—Not yet. Fifteen minutes . . . Don't take him any presents. Harry's never seemed to learn to accept compliments gracefully. Can't think why . . . Fifteen minutes?
—Well, I'll need to find the market first. It'll probably be nearer an hour. . .
—Good luck, Gordon. I'll not say goodbye. We're going to be good friends. Better not say allies. Wait to see how Harry is before you mention coming to see me. Can't have jealousy between you over an old frump like me, can we?
—I'll make sure of that. You're no frump, Margaret. . .
With a lighter step and a brighter eye, Gordon Laird makes for the seventh-floor lift.

☆

Almost before he's half-way across the ill-kept square, Fred sees that Harry's street door has been propped open. He dances a brief jig around an almond tree that's struggling into leaf. He swirls his loaded duffel bag around his head as though practising the sling shot. Half his problem has been solved for him. Having quickened his step among the detritus of uncleared leaves, cider bottles and used condoms, he realises, on reaching the street itself, that there's no further need to hurry.
Mr Duke, the downstairs tenant, is having a clear-out. Around the dustbins are heaps of old discs, a wind-up gramophone, newspaper supplements commemorating the jubilees and deaths of monarchs, and three plastic sacks of Christmas cards. There's a festive touch as well, perhaps not exactly suited to a spring afternoon. Lengths of artificial creepers, in autumnal tones of lemon, apricot, and plum hang, like festoons, on the dustbins.
As Fred picks over this plastic kitsch, and the assortment that lies around, he weighs up what might be of interest to his market contacts, and what might come in handy. He's interrupted by

a deep wheezing from the doorway. Mr Duke rests a dozen lengths of plastic bamboo against the porch and fights to gain control of breath.

Fred nods his head and offers a friendly wink.

–Nice to see you again. What's all the bamboo, then? Building a sampan in case we get more rain?

–Eh? . . . What? . . . Oh, it's you, is it? . . . Sampan? Got enough Chinese round here already . . . Was you looking for a room, wasn't it? Find anything?

–Above your very head, believe it or not.

–Upstairs? Well, there's a change in the weather. What's Mr Plimsoll going to do for a consulting room, then? What's to happen to all these hard-luck cases he lets doss down overnight? . . . Not having me on, are you?

–What d'you think this is? . . . Started bringing some gear over. . .

–Bet he's charging you the earth. . .

–Wouldn't say that. We've come to an arrangement, Harry and me. The name's Fred, by the way.

–And I'm Mr Duke.

–Care to guess what I've got in this pocket?

–Nothing you've nicked, I hope. We're respectable round here.

–Yeah, Harry told me you've got politicians all down the main road . . . These are bulbs, see? Gardening's my line, Mr Duke. All these dropped off a table. Straight up, they did.

–No use to me, mate.

–Enjoy looking at them, won't you, when they come up? Gladioli . . . dahlias etc. I'll need to stick these in before it gets dark. I took a look out the back from upstairs. It's not big, I grant you. Got potential though. . .

–You'll need to do a bit of hard digging to get anywhere. That tree out the back's an ash. Kills anything. Mrs Duke tried. . .

–I've got plans for that ash . . . Look, mustn't hold you up. I'll dump this gear upstairs and then get cracking . . . Could you use a couple of lamb chops? There'll be plenty for Harry and me . . . Got a mate in Smithfield, see?

–Well, that's very kind of you, I'm sure. Doing the cooking, too?

–When I'm around. Don't like rotas . . . Harry not about?

–Went out around two, he did. I just happened to hear the door bang.
–Hope he doesn't wear himself out. I was thinking of dragging him off to a disco tonight. . .
–Him? Mr Plimsoll? He'd never endure all that noise thudding in his ears. All I ever hear's classical stuff. If the windows happen to be open, that is. . .
–You'll see. It's spring, Mr Duke. Time to get the blood moving . . . Right. Here's your chops . . . Mind if I take a squint through all this lot, later on? . . . Tell you what, I could use these bits of creeper. . .
–Plastic creepers in the garden? . . . Not getting gnomes, are you? Mrs Duke couldn't abide gnomes. Said they all looked like Wilson and Heath.
–No gnomes. Gardens must look natural. That's lesson number one . . . I've got other ideas for these creepers.

☆

The phone in the lounge stops ringing while Harry, at the bottom of the stairs, continues to shuffle through letters that have been there, unopened, for three days. He tears up outdated news releases and pockets an invitation. The electricity bill and the income tax demand he carries with him to the lounge, and throws into the waste bin.

Without bothering to pull off his shoes, he stretches himself along the couch and opens a new pack of cigarettes. With every intention of resolving exactly what is to be done about Fred, he finds that his head still echoes with things said by Dave, the cyclist. The actual words have slipped already but the concepts persist. Dave's simple pleasure in young Sean's company, regardless of tragedy tomorrow, or the next day, is beyond irritation. It is the raw material of a sad farce. Dave seems a man unable to realise he's setting himself up for a revival of *Death in Venice*.

Harry gets up impatiently and pours himself a king-size glass of sherry. He needs no one to remind him of the parallel between

Dave and Sean, and Harry Plimsoll and Fred. Accepting the age difference between a twenty-three-year-old and a man of forty-plus is narrower than that between a schoolboy and someone in his late twenties, Harry is very sure he'd be cast by Fred as a teacher: that role from which he wrenched himself in his own mid-twenties. The apartment would become nothing more than an informal return to the classroom.

And just how long would it last? The cards would be stacked, at first, in the teacher's favour. No matter how deftly they might be played, time would not be on the teacher's side. Like Sean, like Tadzio himself, Fred would grow up. Harry takes a good mouthful of sherry and develops a fantasy. He sketches out *Death in Venice: Part Two. Tadzio's First Shave.* Aschenbach-Plimsoll does not succumb to cholera. It was merely a mild heart attack on the beach. The world's first pacemaker is implanted. Aschenbach-Plimsoll and Tadzio-Fred gambol through the lagoons, the ice-cream parlours of St Mark's Square, and over the damask covers of a gilded bed. And then? . . . Tadzio's first shave. The final sequence is inevitable. Tadzio-Sean-Fred kisses his mentor a light goodbye, and skips off to a disco, even an orgy, on some other stretch of the world's limitless gay beach.

He twirls the sherry glass, surprised that it is empty. The early evening light sparkles against the hand cut crystal. The cyclist's eyes, Harry recalls, sparkled as he talked of coming home. Noreen's eyes brightened when she mentioned Dimitri. Gordon's too, but over-eagerly, and with a wish to please. Fred's? Harry admits they also sparkled, not the first night, but sitting astride the window-box he'd brought.

He's about to refill the glass when the phone rings again. Crossing the lounge, he slams down the window, not to exclude the cooler evening air, but a strong smell of cooking. Harry resolves to have a sharp word with Mr Duke.

–Harry, dear. This is your mother speaking from a telephone with wheels. Well, perhaps I should say on wheels.

–And this, Mother mine, is your only son, back from an exhausting trek through South London. I'm working on a complicated story. If you're going to give me your tear-stained routine about no visitors, remember what I said. Stand on your

own feet, and remember also, I might very well have been out of the country. Right?
–Now, Harry. No need to take it out on me because you're tired and ratty. Don't expect sympathy from me if you've got to face a pile of washing up before you can even start to think about cooking for yourself. Anyway, I was ringing to tell you I *did* have a visitor this afternoon. And a very nice time we had, too. Can you guess who it might have been?
–Batty Aunt Winnie? . . . Mother, I've just this second walked in. I need to relax and then I have to eat. . .
–We all do, Harry. That's what I'm trying to say. I think I've found someone who'd fit very comfortably into that spare room of yours. . .
–What spare room? There isn't one. . .
–How forgetful you can be. I know my illness has been adding to the strain. What I'm saying is, why not get rid of that dreadful commissionaire you've got on the top floor? You need someone who could give you a hand with things. Someone to talk to in the evenings.
–Have they put you on new drugs? What are you raving about? Who have you been talking to, you old She-Wolf?
–Harry. Anyone would think you were accusing me of scheming! I just happened to be talking to that nice boy from Scotland. Gordon, isn't it? He brought me such lovely flowers . . . but we'll let that pass.
–This is too much. I'll not have the two of you cornering me. D'you hear?
–Nobody's cornering you, Harry. I was thinking of you, dear. Gordon's so practical. He can cook. He does woodwork. He'd be so useful about the place. And he'd put you first, Harry. Just as dear John put me.
–He would? So, what would I do? Dress up in drag and play you?
–What's drag, dear?
–Transvestism: the pantomime dame, Vesta Tilley . . . Old Mother Riley. Forget it. I can't stop you and Gordon Laird buttering each other up, but hear this. You can do it outside my house. That clear? I'll have no bloody triangles played here. Matter of fact, there is someone who may be moving in. . .

–Tell me about him. I take it you've a man in mind. . .
–I'll tell you nothing about him. . .
–Just like John. Unwilling to share. Why are you so secretive, Harry?

Harry, about to smash the phone into its receiver, hears the street door-bell ringing. He chooses to ignore it.

–Look at yourself in a mirror and you might just see the answer. Before I ring off, listen . . . Do you hear the door-bell? If that's your messenger boy, Gordon Laird, I've a good mind to open this window so you can hear me tell him to piss off . . . That's what I said, Piss off.

–Such coarse expressions you've picked up from that night-club commissionaire. Harry, listen to me. It doesn't matter if you like doing things with other men. It's always gone on. There was that novelist I used to enjoy. He had fancy men. His wife was insatiable for girls who worked in the hairdresser's. Of course, in public they always appeared together. . .

–Thank you for the liberalism, Mother. I've managed without for years. I'll choose my man and I'll run my life. Understand?

The only comfort for Harry as he tries to end the conversation, on his terms, is that the ringing at the bell has finished.

–But I do understand, Harry. All I'm saying is, if you're inventing this man who might be moving in, you could do far worse than try seeing Gordon again. Have a word with him.

–One word. It'll be No. And two words for you: Good night.

–Isn't that usually written as one word, dear?

Harry bangs down the phone and goes to the window. He opens it and scans the street but there is no sign of Gordon Laird or of anyone else he recognises. The smell of meat being fried is more pungent by the second. He wonders if Mr Duke has died while cooking his evening meal or is at least suffering from amnesia.

With the window closed again, Harry remains, contemplating his reflection in the glass. How much more substantial is it, he asks himself, than any relationship? What can anyone count on? He thinks of the eighteen years of Gordon's life, curtailed by one unexpected squall at the mouth of the Thames. He sets against this the simple enjoyment of Dave, the cyclist, outlining a daily pleasure in the here and now. And his thoughts revert to Fred, just as assertive and independent as himself, listing achievable delight.

Harry realises that his head has turned and he is looking left towards the main road. It is the direction from which Fred should come. Whether the attraction that he now admits is mutual will last, he doesn't care. Maybe it will still be there on the day when the wrinkles round Fred's eyes don't fade with a joke they've exchanged. Perhaps it will not be important that Fred's breath will not always smell as young as he sleeps on the next pillow. All that, Harry concludes, is as trivial as tomorrow when compared with Fred's zest for enjoying the affordable pleasures of today.

–He is my Australia. My insurance against drifting with Gordon into the suburbs of middle age. The only price tag he'll insist on is that I value him as a person, not as some extension of myself. He's no piano or bedside phone. And if he quits next week, it'll have been worth it. He'll not tidy me up, like Gordon . . . Unlike you, dear Margaret, he'll allow me a private space . . . It's a risk; what isn't? If I'm to share it again with anyone, then so be it, I choose Fred.

But there's still no Fred, whistling along from the corner. The newspaper stall has been closed for the night, and a park-keeper is evicting a couple of lads with their bed rolls. In Harry's lounge, the smell of onions frying is over-powering. He plans a tirade against Mr Duke.

Out on the landing, and ready to bound down the stairs in fury, Harry encounters a cloud of smoke erupting from the kitchen.

–What the hell is going on?

As though evoked from an underworld, Fred appears in the doorway and grins. He is almost naked. A short garland of plastic creeper is twined round his sweaty forehead. A second, rather longer, serves as an allusion to a jock-strap. His cheeks reddened partly by heat from the stove, and partly from a flask of wine, are like ripe pomegranates. He still holds the flask of chianti in one hand. In the other he has a toasting fork on which what remains of a lamb chop is impaled.

He offers the chianti to Harry.

–How the hell did you get in?

–Thank Grandpa Duke downstairs. What d'you reckon to the gear, Harry?

Harry does like what little there is of it. A more total randiness than he's experienced for years grips him. He likes Fred's cocky wink, he likes the mud from the garden still adhering to his arms. Most of all, he likes Fred's careless sensuality. Feeling the need to say something, he makes a suggestion without meaning one word of it.

–You need a bath.

–All in good time, Honey Bear. It's been a hard day among the tulips. Out the back there, too, come to think of it. Grub was uppermost. Thought you might fancy a lamb chop . . . Picked up some bits and pieces for us on the way home. . .

Us, already, Harry thinks. Home . . . So soon?

Fred seizes the chianti and downs a generous gulp. As he flips the chops and then prods at the onions, he hops from left foot to right, gyrating his hips. He knows exactly what he's doing to me, Harry says to himself. He's going to stick all that fry-up in the oven in less than one minute from now, and we both understand what's going to happen then.

Harry takes the flask again and lets wine pour into his mouth and down onto his chin like an overflowing fountain. Having emptied his mouth, he puts a question in as unconcerned a tone as he can manage.

–Did you hear the bell? . . . I was on the phone. . .

–Yeah. I coped . . . that bloke's a boring fart, Harry.

–Mr Duke? He doesn't often ring. . .

–No, not Grandpa Duke . . . That bloke from Scotland. Half-pissed again, as usual. Know what? He tried to pick me up the night I met you . . . I told him downstairs he'd missed his chance with me. And with you, come to that.

–You did, did you? . . . Hang on . . . You didn't go to the door like that? Naked?

–Why not? It's only like those soldiers on your towel, isn't it? I don't have a helmet, mind.

–But what about people who might have been passing?

–What about 'em, Harry? I've got nothing to be ashamed of. It's not exceptional but it's what I was born with. I don't know of any swop shop. Anyway, I told him you weren't in.

–Suppose I'd wanted to see him?
–Harry! What's he got for you? Hang on while I strain these spuds. Mind if I use an egg when I mash 'em? Makes it smoother in the mouth, you might say. . .

Fred winks once more as he passes Harry, emphasising the overtone. Harry smiles, while thinking that it is probably better for Gordon to have met Fred. It might do something to sever a few more strands of the mesh that's been binding him.

–Did Gordon say what he wanted?
–Nothing that'll do you any good, that's for sure. I've seen looks like that before. Some lawyer up Oldham way, he had that look. Not come to bed so much as let's settle down and be comfy. That'd be bad for you, Harry . . . What's his name? Gordon? Yeah, Gordon'd have you middle-aged and pulling the Christmas crackers in no time . . . Now me, I'd. .
–Want to drag me round the discos and through half the camping grounds of Europe?
–Less of the camping. I know what it means . . . Well, we might do a disco later. Got a mate who's on the door of one place. He'll pass us in free . . . I put the oven on low. Give us time to have another go at that chianti.
–Did Gordon say if he'd come back?
–Shouldn't think he would. I told him to go and loosen up in a commune. Forget him, Harry. Don't join the undead. Here, have a swig. You look about as lively as Brighton in November.

All the food, most of it overcooked, is in the oven. Fred turns to Harry, begins his disco dance again and waggles his index fingers less distance than a breath from Harry's nipples.

–Fred, it's time to eat! Stop it! Who do you think you are? Dionysus?
–Who's he? You and your long words. I'm Fred. . .

Harry tries one last bluster though he knows the opening game is over and has ended in a draw.

–I just don't know, Fred. I'm still not sure we're right for each other. . .
–Got message from the Holy Ghost on the phone, did you?
–Fred, be serious. Well, I don't know why we should be serious. All I'm saying is, I'm old enough to be your father. . .

–So who says that doesn't turn me on? I've never seen my bloody father. He never held me. No man I ever wanted to ever has. Just you, Honey Bear.

Harry clenches his fists and closes his eyes. It's the only way he can prevent himself leaning slightly to lick a rill of sweat that's dampening the dozen hairs on Fred's chest. When he does open his eyes, it is because Fred has jumped at him, pinning knees against Harry's thighs, and clasping both arms round Harry's neck. There's just a moment for Harry to look into eyes that are lit with delight and affection, before Fred wrinkles his nose and moves closer, waggling his tongue.

–Fred, shouldn't we eat first?

–It'll be there later. Or tomorrow. Want you Harry. Now. . .

Disengaging himself, Fred grabs the kitchen towel and spreads it on the floor. With sure movements, and between kisses, he removes Harry's jersey and rolls it into a pillow.

☆

His left side warmed by Fred's limbs, his right chilled by night air from the open window, Harry stirs, shifts his head and at last focuses on the sound of the phone. He gropes for his watch, misses, and it falls from the table edge into a puddle of chianti near Fred's thigh. Cursing quietly, he draws the window down and pads across to the lounge.

–It's Harry Plimsoll. . .

–Hello, Harry . . . Were you asleep? . . . It isn't that late in London, is it?

–Who is this?

–Who do you think? . . . Don't I sound like Noreen?

–Noreen! . . . Yes . . . yes, of course. Sorry. I was having a nap . . . Long day and all that bit . . . Did you miss your plane or something? . . . You sound too close for Athens, or wherever. . .

–Might have been better if I had missed my plane. Look, Harry, there's a crisis on. . .

–You mean there's been a coup?

–Come on, Harry. Wake up. I mean a personal crisis. The police have just contacted me . . . Harry, my mother is dead.

Still yawning, but doing his best to concentrate, Harry murmurs a phrase or so of sympathy and asks if he can help in any way. He suggests an immediate visit to Richmond if there's anything urgent to be done.

–No, that's not necessary, but thanks all the same. The neighbours are coping. It's a question of finding Ricky. Frankly, I don't know where to start. He was in London twelve hours ago, that I do know . . . I'm still all mixed up, Harry . . . I'll be back tomorrow as soon as they can get me on a plane. Bang goes all my holiday money. . .

–At least you've got Dimitri. . .

–Yes? . . . One night with Dimitri'll be worse than none at all . . . Anyway, about Ricky. I'm not trying to burden you with anything, Harry. Really I'm not. You're the only one I could think of. Hospital Registry gave me your number . . . I just thought . . . with your journalist's contacts . . . What I'm saying is, I don't want the police looking for him. . .

–Yes. See what you mean . . . Won't be easy, Noreen. London's bursting with kids traipsing through Carnaby Street all day, then up and down the King's Road till dawn. All I know of your son is, he's in his twenties, called Ricky . . . Woodward, isn't it? . . . and he may or may not have a Thames Valley accent. Not a lot to go on.

–Look, Harry. I'd better tell you. I still call him Ricky. We invented it when he was a child. For my sake, as much as anything. I couldn't bear to be reminded of the bloody mountie. Maybe if I stopped thinking of him as Ricky, we'd be in a bit closer contact. Anyway. . .

–Come on, Noreen. You did all you could, I'm sure. Stop wasting good drinking time with the psychology. What's the lad's name?

–Frederick. It was all part of the deal with the mountie to get a good severence and good riddance. If Ricky had been a girl, he'd have been Frederica . . . Now, find me a twenty-three-year-old, about your height, nut-brown hair . . . and my smile. He answers only to the name of Fred. Never Ricky. Find him and I'll love you for ever . . . as the brother I never had.

The pause is so long that Noreen begins to wonder if the line's been cut.

–No . . . I'm still here, Noreen . . . I was . . . jotting it all down . . . Look, leave this with me, will you? . . . No need for you to sit talking to me. Waste of money when you've got other things on your mind. Why not go back to Dimitri and make a night of it? . . . Ring me again on this number when you get back tomorrow. . .

–Harry, you're great. Think you might have some news for me then?

–Yes, Noreen . . . There's a very good chance I'll have something to tell you. Try and have some kind of an evening. See you.

He sits on the carpet by the phone. What he has heard seems to alter so much and yet alters nothing. Noreen has her life. Fred is her son but is also an adult entitled to a life that includes affection. And that, Harry thinks, is what he'll get from me.

Fred, rubbing his eyes, comes into the lounge.

–Hi. . .

–Sorry if I woke you, Fred. Should have closed the door.

–Not important. Woke up, and there you were – gone. Thought you were worried about something. . .

–No. Not now . . . How about that supper? . . . Don't frown. There's nothing to worry about. I'll tell you later. First things first . . . Come over here. . .

–By the window? Thought you were worried about people in the street. . .

–Who cares about them? Come on. . .

☆

FORTHCOMING FROM THIRD HOUSE (PUBLISHERS)

March 1991

DOG DAYS, WHITE KNIGHTS

a collection of essays by David Rees on travel, books, music, gay life and AIDS.

ISBN 1 870188 16 0 £5.50/$9.50

July 1991

TALKING TO. . .

a collection of interviews spanning a quarter of a century between Gay Times' features editor Peter Burton and twenty-five gay writers, including Orton, Isherwood, Kramer and Gale.

ISBN 1 870188 18 7 £5.95/$9.95